Artificially Sweet Delinquent

Sabrina Eiya Makein

authorHOUSE®

AuthorHouse™
1663 Liberty Drive
Bloomington, IN 47403
www.authorhouse.com
Phone: 1 (800) 839-8640

This is a work of fiction. All of the characters, names, incidents,
organizations, and dialogue in this novel are either the products
of the author's imagination or are used fictitiously.

Published by AuthorHouse 04/24/2015

ISBN: 978-1-5049-0567-1 (sc)
ISBN: 978-1-5049-0566-4 (e)

Library of Congress Control Number: 2015905715

Print information available on the last page.

Any people depicted in stock imagery provided by Thinkstock are models,
and such images are being used for illustrative purposes only.
Certain stock imagery © Thinkstock.

This book is printed on acid-free paper.

Because of the dynamic nature of the Internet, any web addresses or
links contained in this book may have changed since publication and
may no longer be valid. The views expressed in this work are solely those
of the author and do not necessarily reflect the views of the publisher,
and the publisher hereby disclaims any responsibility for them.

Contents

For my readers. For everyone.
I love you.
XOXO
Sabrina

Other published books, and soon to be published books, written by Sabrina Eiya Makein:

"The Underestimated Arts of AfriAsia." Published

"Ieda: 45 days a War Child." Coming soon

PROLOGUE

(Always read the prologue. Always.)

BEVERLEY'S INTRODUCTION

It's easy to say that nothing matters—when you have a broken heart. Here I am with a life that even I can't validate because everything I've been through feels like yesterday's dream smothered in a haze of tomorrow. I've never been too certain anyway since I've learned that tomorrow is never promised. The truth is: I've kicked and I've been pushed by certain obstacles—yet I still stand—why? Honestly, *I don't know*. My life is a journey, not an ordinary one, not one of the *inevitable* ones; otherwise I would've identified the end-result. Look, we've spent hours and days, even years, battling ourselves only to wind up in a maze. My maze was entrapped within a foreign maze. My point? Escaping a battle, my battle, that has only just lead to *another* clash, that of which I'm completely and utterly, and without doubt, oblivious to.

Beverley Whatman—my name. That's about it. Everything else is jumbled and rustled in a way that even

I can't seem to exclaim at the very realization of it. I've been blind and sighted; a thief and a liar; a fake; a lost; a delinquent who is undeniably attracted to and intrigued by the *artificially sweet*.

I dream, I tumble, I trip and, yes, I do fall. And, in the midst of it all, I've seem to manifest (right choice of diction here?) into this exquisite, yet abominable, creature of mankind. Am I crazy? I'm not sure, although I'd knowingly stick a label on my head that reads: *Artificially Sweet Delinquent*.

CHAPTER ONE

When we reminisce of Yesterday

"Why are you *alone* here?" A distinctly practiced voice behind me whispered. I tried to stare but I couldn't see anything. Nothing. Everything was dark, but the only thing really clear to me was *my* perception of the world— of this park. But that wasn't much either. "Are you deaf?" she muttered. "No." I whispered as I continued to stare at my visual image of this person speaking at me. I sat alone in the park because it calms my mind. There really isn't much that I can do. I haven't made any friends. Naught. "What's your name?" she asked as I inhaled her perfume. "Is your hand in front of me?" I asked while quickly pushing myself aback. "So, you *are* blind?" That was a rude question, but my lack of sight was bound to be questioned. "Who are you?" I slowly asked. Although I couldn't see her, I pretended not to be afraid. "You still haven't answered *my* question. Are you blind?" I hardly understood her hostility or her sense of humor—if she had any, but I still answered anyway: "I think so."

"Well, that's sad now isn't it? Being blind and having no one to really look up to." That was the stupidest thing I've ever heard. But I couldn't tell her that. I didn't want to decrease my chance of befriending her, funny enough.

"Uh, it's alright, I guess." "What's your name?" she asked as the sound of her popped bubblegum sent shivers down my spine. "Beverley." "I'm Amanda." I liked her name a lot. I wish mine was Amanda. "Do you want to play-around?" What did she mean? "I don't know. What game?" I hesitantly asked. "Well, maybe truth or dare? Or something like that…"

"It's easy and fun. *Trust me.*" She continued.

I was oblivious to whom she was and yet I *did* trust her. "So, truth or dare?" I smiled and said, "truth." "Have you ever kissed a boy?" Silence then quickly altered my mind. I didn't have an answer. It took me a while to reply. I don't even know why I just sat there…blind and empty. "On the lips, you mean?" I whispered. "No, like the real thing—you know? *Kiss.* With the tongue—" I squeezed my face as though I ate a lemon. "Eew! No way." "No need to make a face about it. Well have you *kissed* at all? Ever?" I'd roll my eyes if I could and if she could even see it. "Never, and I fear that I shan't ever." "Oh don't say that. You'll do it someday…soon." I wasn't about to question her intentions. She *was* peculiar. I was afraid of her. She's talking to me, not at me anymore… I'm so afraid. What did she want? Whatever it was I just won't surrender it quickly. Or so I thought… "I've never really carried a conversation with someone like you—being blind and all." I then exhaled the air that I've inhaled out of fear. "Really?" I asked.

"So where do you live?" Mother taught me better than to navigate *strangers* to our home. "Here." I said. "Well, me too. Now isn't that cute?" My hand then randomly lifted and touched her face. She just stood there and accepted it. I touched her face slowly as I began to visualize her appearance. "You're beautiful." I said as I began to giggle. Thank—you." she nervously replied. "Sometimes I wish I *were* blind. At least I wouldn't have to see the world as it is. So much pain and agony—prejudiced minds here and there." "But even the blind can see pain and agony. We can feel it." I said. "Let's be friends." she gasped. I've never felt as happy as the day Amanda exhaled those words to me. *'Let's be friends'* changed me. From that day nothing was ever the same again.

I was only eighteen and yet it felt as though my life was *just* about to begin. I was ready. I wanted it all and right now was best. Amanda came here for a reason. That's what I thought. That's exactly what I wanted to believe. I would've confided in my mother, but I was afraid she would keep Amanda away from me. Mother never wanted me to be happy. Maybe she was afraid that I'd get hurt—I don't know. I'll keep Amanda to myself. Almost like a figment of my own imagination; she will be *mine*. Before meeting Amanda at the park, my life was ridiculously boring. You know how they say, 'boredom kills?' Well, I was at the edge of being squeezed into a coffin. I always pleaded to be home-schooled but mother sent me to this private school where kids don't, and wouldn't ever, give a bollocks about causing pain for and to another person. I was shunned by all of them, because I read "special books" for the blind—books that consisted of unique symbols and *letters*—it's actually called Braille. I was rejected because of my being blind. They never understood my situation, they never tried and they never tried to try.

At times I wanted to end it all. Ironically I wanted to grace 'darkness' even though I was already almost living in darkness. All I ever wanted was happiness. That's all. Nothing more and, really, nothing less. I'll just say that Amanda entered my life—in good timing. I'm hoping that *that* will make sense to you. I wanted to see her right now. She's become a sudden addiction—a disease, and I hardly know *her*. I didn't even ask for her "nationality" or anything like that...not even her age. "What are you doing, darling?" my mother asked as I stood by my bedroom window. I knew what it was because it's where I usually am—when I'm at home. It's almost as though I can see what's outside, although I really wish I could. The window allows me to enter a world where my thoughts are utterly priceless... to me. "Bev?" "Yes, mother?" she then walked to me and began to brush my hair. "Frederick will be home tonight, since I have a party to attend." I *resented* Frederick. He was the worst brother ever conceived of. I can't stay a night with *him*—I shan't! "I can't leave you alone." 'Yes you can. I'm not a child." Maybe I was, but I'd rather fight for my right than be babysat by Frederick. "Sorry. You have no choice." I then pouted my lips as though to kiss someone—I wish. "*That* will make you ugly someday." mother said as she referred to the pout. "I'm already ugly isn't it—" before I could even complete my sentence, mother's words echoed in my head before they were said: "Your beauty is desired by most girls. Your generosity is envied by all." She always said *that* whenever I doubted myself.

Before she left she pecked my cheek with her Chanel lipgloss. I could almost see the color. I know it was red but I wanted to actually *see* it; to know what *red* really was. "One day, Beverley, a miracle will happen, baby. One day." my blind tears dropped down my cheek as I stood there speechless.

I spent the day by the window, waiting for Amanda. I expected her to know my residence—I don't know why. I stood there, but she didn't come. Maybe she was busy. I just didn't want to be alone with Frederick—I didn't trust him. I lost my appetite from the thought of him. He was just evil. Utterly disgusting and I was ashamed to refer to him as my "blood." I wanted to run-away somewhere where I'd be the only existing thing. Just for a while.

"Anybody home?" Frederick's voice from downstairs shook the floor upstairs. I didn't want to reply so I climbed into bed and pretended to be asleep. I wanted nothing to do with him. I had a choice. Hearing the knock on the door *somehow* squeezed my eyes-shut. As it opened, my heart began to race. 'Not again,' I thought to myself. "Oh." he whispered—almost as though he read my mind. He shut the door without further intentions of interrupting my *sleep*. I wish it was always like this.

I began to reminisce on the day I was born; what I felt and anything else that I could remember. All I wanted was to clarify my mind—completely seclude thoughts of Frederick.

Thinking of the children at school and my neighborhood didn't brighten my mood either. And then I remembered it: the day when I wished I wasn't born.

I'd never forget it. Frederick was there—I'd never forget. I shook my head as though to erase the memory, but it shall forever remain. It's a scar that I must live with for the rest of my life. I was afraid.

At times he would invite his spineless friends here, and then I'd stay in my room. Almost like a prisoner of some sort. At times I'd pray that death would take him. It's all I wanted. It's insanity that mother can't seem to understand my feelings—that I don't find comfort in Frederick's presence. I can't seem to explain it to her and it's not that I would. But she should feel it...at least by now. So I just laid there, on my bed, paying attention to my memories of Yesterday.

"Beverley, open the window." I knew that it was Amanda. But what was her business here, right now—it's late. I walked to her with a smirk planted on my face, opened the window and whispered, "what're you doing here?" "I missed you, mate." We haven't known each other long enough and yet we felt close. "Shall we go out?" she confidently asked. I then bit my lip as I thought about mother. She would kill me if I left. "Are you crazy?" "Yes." *We both were in a way.*

"Just live your life!" Amanda shrieked. "Shhh, my brother is downstairs." "So, *that's* your brother? The one shagging a girl on the sofa?" Alright, so Frederick always got his way, somehow. "Serious?" I asked as Amanda climbed into my room. "You know, it doesn't have to be

12

this way." She said. I was oblivious as to what her current intentions were. I'm not certain I wanted to know… "You don't need to be here." "Why? You hardly know me anyway." "Don't be so quick to *judge*." "I can help you." she said as she *threw herself* on my bed. "Help? I'm okay as it is." "Positive?" I just stood there *staring* into space.

"You know, we all need *someone*." She laughed. "What do you want?" her laughter scared me. She was just peculiar—indeed. My *eyes* remained glued on her direction as I began to wonder *who she really* was. "Where are you from?" There was no reply. She just *laid* there staring at the ceiling, I guess. Did she hear that? "I don't know." "How can you not know where—" "Listen, I just don't know. Even if I did, is it important?" she attacked. From that moment on I failed to utter another word to her regarding her nationality.

"Let's just hang in my room, if you want." "Literally?" she joked as I shook my head. We spent the day, and night, speaking about my life…my life, not hers. It was as though she had no life. I stared at her *green eyes*. *She was fit—sexy*, actually. I felt an attraction between us, but I think it's just a 'girl thing' isn't it? Every time she spoke her words echoed in my head. Sweet echoes really. I could only stare and smile. How peculiar. I anticipated the moment she would mention her family, or anything like that. Perhaps a brief description of her childhood— but naught. She hardly exhaled a sentence regarding her 'family.' I assumed she had one—everyone has one, and I know she's from *somewhere*; aren't we all?

"You look—lost." And lost I was. Thinking of *her* history, and actually making up answers to my own questions about her left me completely lost—for a moment. "Shall I go?" I quickly grabbed her wrist and said, "no. Please stay." *Her energy* was rather appealing. She then *smiled* and whispered, "so you want me to *stay* the night?" That really *would* be the cherry on top of my cake—really. I had no desire of being alone, today, and neither will I tomorrow. I nodded my head like a child agreeing with their parent to be good for the night. "Alright. This ought to be fun." Amanda convincingly muttered.

"So what do you do all day?" "Nothing much. Homework and stuff." "No worries, I'm here now." I wanted to confide in her, but I'd never. I couldn't. And on top of that I hardly know her. So, I spent most of the night wondering whether I should, or if I should keep quiet. So I kept quite silent—for the night. "Something bothering you, Bev?" "You know, my situation isn't *easy*. I may come out as a weak chap when really, I am by far, the strongest person I've acknowledged." she then sighed and said, "it's great that you've acknowledged yourself. I'm waiting for me to acknowledge me. Right now I'm only acquainted with myself." and then we both giggled at the thought of sounding like mad people. Well, perhaps we were.

"Do you sometimes wish that you could see things as they were?" I then bowed my head in response to the question I've, somehow, dreaded to hear. "Well?" she said. "At times I wish I were dead you know? So then I wouldn't have to put up with *this*." I then waved my hands around the room and continued: "I haven't seen the real world for years, and I don't want to...I fear the truth." I said as I let out a loud sigh. "Wow. Deep." Even that reply seemed a bit *deep* to me. "I agree. The world is a shithole if you ask me. Even though you're in it, just stay away from others. That's better somehow." I never asked to be here. But now that I'm here I might as well shield myself from the obstacle that could deface my very existence: The truth that is.

"You trust me, right?" Amanda nervously asked. I wondered why she cared but I replied anyway. "Yeah. I do." She exhaled and then cleared her throat. "You hardly know me and you *trust me*?" "Big deal, right?" "I could be a killer or something, Bev." "If you were, then I'd beg you to teach me." "To kill?!" I then nodded. "I knew there *was* something about *you*, Bev."

Ditto, Amanda...Ditto.

Summertime never felt more exciting. For the first time, ever, I anticipated the next day. I knew that Amanda would make it interesting, and I began to love her. Every summer before this was excruciatingly boring and repetitive. Since I never really had friends and my mother had a job; Frederick and his friends were usually here. Most of the time I'd be at the park; where I could be myself. I'd always plant a phantom smile in the presence of others—I couldn't let them know that I hurt. Somehow I feared the fact that they would use it against me. People are strange—we have funny ways of looking at things. But Amanda was different. She's just what I needed, all this time. You know; sometimes it's the small details in life that truly complement our entire existence. Mine is Amanda...or so I believed.

"Do you have secrets?" We all do. But mine is just a bit darker than others. "Yes. But I'll only share if you share." she said. "There's nothing that I *have* to share." "Then neither will I." she whispered. Sometimes a strong shield is obligatory otherwise people will stomp all over you, and then probably wipe you to the side. I wasn't quite ready for that. "Well, just know that you can confide in me." Amanda said. I knew that I could. For some reason I really had no doubt in my mind. Amanda was what I needed all this time. She's finally *here with me*. Time was moving quite fast and I hated it. I wanted more *time* with Amanda, almost as though we were lovers. Well, we kind of are now aren't we? Not in *that* way but in a *friendly* way. I can finally speak without doubting myself; Amanda and I can learn from each other; we can grow together. I've never had something or someone like this before. Amanda was here to save me—from my mind. My own little secret she will be. No one else will take her away. Just the thought of her befriending someone else fazed me. *Amanda was mine. Mine alone; and that's it.*

"Your eyes—" she paused and continued. "They're unique. Beautiful. Different." Was that a compliment or not? I've never had someone compliment my eyes. Maybe it's out of sympathy or something. I hoped not... "Thanks." I shyly replied with my bowed head. "Don't do *that*." "What?" "Shy away. Show them that you're confident and that you're proud—of what you are." Of *what* I was? "Alright then." "The kids at your school.

What're they like?" Well, they're human just like us. They're rude; some are promiscuous—others are convicts and the rest are saints—quite likely. "They're normal. I guess." I said. "They tease you, don't they? They seclude you from their lives as though *they're* kings and queens, isn't it?" The more she spoke the more I felt inspired. I wish I met her before; either way—she was there. That's all that mattered.

"How about your school?" I asked as she giggled as though my question was amusing. Raising my eyebrow must've signaled my *seriosity*. "I don't go." I wish I never had *to go* to school too. This seemed unfair but we all live separate lives. "Why—may I ask?" "*Woman*! Too many questions. Take it as it is." My jaw suddenly dropped as though she insulted me. It was a simple question but I just took it *as it was*. "So, you, literally, can't see anything? Not even a blur?" It was alright for her to question me but I couldn't do the same? Insanity. "Naught." I replied. "I'm going to sleep." she quickly mumbled. She probably figured that I was irritated. I sat there, imagining her sleep, and I felt safe. Frederick and his girl—friend kept me awake. I couldn't bear the fact that we were under the same roof.

I slowly caressed my face and wondered if I was—*beautiful*. I touched my lips and then squeezed them. I pulled my cheeks as though they were elastic; I must be beautiful too. Mother always told me "everyone is beautiful—in their own way." It's never really *what is inside* that matters—that's what I thought, because no one seems to look *into* my heart anyway. I listened to

Amanda breathe as she slept, or pretended to sleep, and everything suddenly seemed alright. It's the summer of '05 and it shouldn't end...Ever. If I had my way, I'd probably runaway with her. But right now I'll just admire. I began to drift away—sleep conquered me. I was there in that place; where it was only Amanda and I—just the way that it should be.

I awoke to find nothing next to me. Nobody. She wasn't there.

There I was on my own—like before. All I could do was walk toward the window and pretend as though she was standing there—waiting for me. I could hear mother speaking downstairs and Frederick's voice. I stayed in my room until it felt safe to go downstairs. There really wasn't much that I could do. Amanda was gone and the least I could do was look in the bathroom—maybe she was there. But I chose not to. I already knew...She was gone. "Beverley!" my mother yelled. I ignored. Amanda was on my mind and she's all I wanted. "Beverley!" I continued to ignore. I remained by the window as though I were a statue. *Beverley* was not ready to move—anywhere. Amanda could've waited for me, she could've. Why didn't she? Where is she anyway? "Why didn't you answer me?" I quickly turned around and smiled. "Oh, I didn't hear you, mother." She was probably hoping that I didn't lose my sense of hearing...that would be a complete tragedy now, wouldn't it? A deaf and blind daughter. Next I would be mute...Then my life would be completely and utterly over.

"I'm leaving to the mall. Would you like to join me?" I placed my head on my forehead and exhaled a lie. "Actually, I'm not feeling too well. I think I'll stay home." "You must be hungry. There's food in the kitchen; oh and Fred left. His girlfriend was here—" she paused and coughed. "I don't fancy her" she said. I didn't either and I haven't even met her. I just smiled at mother as she walked away. I knew that Amanda would be here soon—I didn't know when but I was waiting. I quickly showered and then ate breakfast. Crepes with honey and orange juice—delicious. I listened to some of John Mayer's songs—heavenly. Especially "bigger than my body." Somehow that song directly changes my mood. I might meet him in the future—hopefully.

"Pssst, darling. How are you?" Amanda whispered from my kitchen-window. How did she know I was *here*? Awkward but lovely. "Amanda!" I yelled. Almost like a child in a toy-store really. But I didn't care. I was glad she came...I knew she would. "Eating without me?" "You just left me. Why?" she then giggled and said, "I'm sorry, husband. I never meant to *just leave*. Next time I'll leave the divorce papers." she teased. We both then laughed. She ate as well, and told me how much she loved John Mayer—something *major* that we have in common. "He's extremely sexy, that one. What *is it* about him?" "I don't know." It was probably the fact that he had talent; a brain and *looks*. Definitely...

"Listen. I want to show you something." She whispered gently. Usually when people say that, don't they mean, 'I've done something wrong and you're my alibi.' I don't know, I've just always thought of it like that—yet I still took a risk. "Show me what?" "Come with me." She said. I didn't think twice we just swiftly walked away. Moments later, I heard noises and I knew we were in the street or something. This felt wrong—I didn't like it. "Beverley, have you ever wanted something so bad that you would do anything to get it?" I knew something was wrong. "What?" she grabbed my hand and said, "help me." I knew it. It's either about stealing or killing. "All you need to do is—" "Amanda. What are you doing?" "Bev, we're friends—right?" I couldn't stand the chance of losing her. "Yes." I quickly replied with sweat dropping down my forehead. I've never done something like this—ever. But, maybe it was because I never really had the chance—or since nobody else would risk their lives doing things like this with *me.* "I'll direct you. Just listen to me."

I was a fool but then again which loner wouldn't be? I made a friend and I wasn't ready to lose her—just yet. "What are we *taking*?" I whispered. "Darling. We're not *taking*, really. We're buying." It was obviously a lie that I chose to believe. She then took my hand and my heart began to race. What would my mother say? What if we got caught? *Jesus.* Your palms are sweaty—relax will you?" My breathing slowly decreased and suddenly I was set. "Just relax and we won't get caught." She's done this before—it's probably her daily routine. Somehow, deep in my heart, I knew that I enjoyed this moment.

I felt alive—when did that *ever* occur? Never. So I just graced the moment. I could sense people stare at me; at us. "There in that corner." She whispered. "Where?" "Just walk ahead and touch every fabric on that rack until you feel a *satin* fabric-ish dress."

"Aren't you coming?" I asked as I began to hesitate. "It *will be* obvious, don't you think? Take this bag and shove the dress in there. It's satin; remember."

I slowly swallowed spit and began to walk. I could sense her watching me but I couldn't turn around. Not that I could see her anyway. I reached my hand to the clothes and brushed through each one until—I found it: The satin-ish fabric, I thought to myself. My hand embraced it as though it were mine. I didn't have a plan. I just stood there with a dress on my hand—a dress for Amanda. Someone must've spotted me. The camera's are around—they *must have* surveillance here, right? I moved around as though I was in search of something. I *was* actually—in search of something. Maybe a sign that I'll survive this? "In the bag." I heard Amanda mumble. It's as easy for her to direct as it is for me to drop this garment and walk away. And I did it. I *shoved* it in the Chanel bag that I knew my mother loved so much. I could almost hear Amanda smile—I could sense her happiness. I had to navigate away before I was seen. "Hand it over. I'll deal with it from here." Amanda said. She went somewhere and returned minutes later sounding happier. "Alright. Shall we go?" "But the alarm." "Fuck the alarm, darling. We've already done this." For some reason I was naive enough to believe her and before I knew it we arrived back home—safely. "We made it?" "*Obviously*. I told you it was alright."

"Now I have a Jane Norman dress." My jaws dropped. "Serious? You made me steal at Jane Norman?" "Oh big deal. Gucci will be next." she teased. "Beverley, life is so short and the luxurious life isn't affordable." "To me it is."

"Well tough." she opened the fridge and grabbed something. "What did you do in the shop? Like when you left me." I asked.

"Nothing" she replied as she loudly flicked the lid on the soda can. "If you listen to me you'll be alright. I'm *your* friend." I didn't agree with the *insidious intentions* and adrenaline-rush, but the aftermath felt damn good. "Movie?" "Yes. Are you hungry?" "Pizza time." Amanda was *clearly* the boss. I knew that listening to her meant having a life and a life is exactly what I needed—wanted.

*"He quickly tossed me around; right on all fours.
My face—opposite the window."*

Watching "Breakfast at Tiffany's" for the umpteenth time while awaiting our pizza felt ravishing—sort of. Mother always watched this movie and explained it to me: I fell in love with it too. Amanda talked most of the time as she laid back on the sofa, the way I usually do? With her feet rested on the arm of the sofa—comfortably. I shan't complain. We laughed at the funny parts and shed a couple of tears at the—not so funny parts. After a while the pizza arrived and Amanda jumped up like a frog, or something. She was hungry—that was clear. She ran toward the door and then I heard, "My—sweet Jesus. You're quite handsome aren't you?" "Who is it, Amanda?" I yelled. The delivery boy obviously flirted back and it was a game until I arrived at the door. Things got a bit—saucy. "Bev, remember last-night's game?" I knew what was next. "Well, I dare *you* to kiss Brian here." "What? Who? No." "Oh come on. Don't be such a pooper." "I'm not a poo—" before I could continue, and I don't know how or when, but Mr. Brian and I kissed.

"See, it's *that* simple. And you're still alive. No pain." I stood there as though I were smacked hard—very hard. "Is your friend *blind*?" he asked. "Yes. Is there a prob?"

"No. I think it's fascinating." Amanda took over as though *her* lips were kissed today. "Well, *fascinate* your way back to Pizza-hut." Amanda ordered him. "*That* pizza isn't free you know?" "Neither was that kiss. Tell your boss and so *will I.*" Amanda yelled before she slammed the door shut. So *that's* the way that she handled things—everything was for free. Has she spent a pound on *anything?* Ever? I was afraid to speak, I don't have a current and solemn death-wish.

The way she ate: It reminded me of myself. Chewing on food as though tomorrow was definitely not coming. What a coincidence. "Yeah I like to slice it in four; fold it and then chew." "I can tell." I said. "Good sense." I tilted my head and asked her, "do you always do *that?*" "That what?" "The *thing* with the delivery boys and Jane Norman." "Oh no darling. *You* did *that.* I only introduced you." She then slammed me right on the forehead with a pillow—inevitable behavior. "Admit that you liked, no, you loved it." she said as she began to tickle me. "Oh stop" I screamed as laughter nearly choked me. She continued tickling. Before I knew it; *smack*, right on the lips. This was all just *too much* for one day. I just stood up; walked to the bathroom and rinsed my mouth. "Didn't you enjoy it? Is it my breath?" Amanda asked. "Girls are *not* really my main interest, *Amanda.*" I could've sworn that I heard her mumble, "we'll see." but I was too scared to ask. What *was* I dealing with? I actually enjoyed that peck...I did, although I had to pretend that it sickened me.

I'm *not* a lesbian right? Right? "Don't worry, you're not a les." I froze as I stared at her. How—how?

"I'm only here to amuse you. I don't abuse; I only amuse. Now bear that in mind." And so I did. As I paid close attention to her every sentence; I began to think: 'Maybe I judge quickly. Shall I wait to see the outcome? Shall I seclude her from my life?' Either way I already knew the answer. Inside me somewhere I already knew that I needed her. Amanda has quickly grasped a part of me—and I'm not certain I want it back. As I sat there battling myself I realized that she was gone. "Amanda?" Silence. So she just disappears whenever she wants? "Yeah?" I heard. Or maybe not. "I love your bathroom—so stylish!" she stopped walking and exclaimed, "I must leave now!" So soon. She couldn't. "I'll be back later, if not—I'll see you tomorrow." All I could do was wave even though I knew I would see her again. There I was alone again awaiting the presence of Amanda. *Again.* She *was* right—she was there to amuse me.

Being alone in *this house* was my resentment. The sounds that haunted me. The visual images that lived in me. I had to bear it all...Alone. There are many questions that mother had to answer—but I was afraid to ask. I feared everything, really, except Amanda. Somehow I knew that I was safe. She *would* keep me safe.

"You shun me in front of my friends. Embarrassment you are. Hideous creature! I wish you were never born. Do you enjoy this? Is this what you want, Beverley? How about me? When will you ever learn? Can you even see that I hurt? It never had to be this way."

I then began to shiver as those words swallowed my mind. I felt goose-bumps on my arms, neck; on my entire body. *It never had to be that way.* Mother never had to leave me alone. I curled up on the sofa and then a tear dropped slowly. No one could see me or feel my pain. No one. Amanda wasn't here now. Amanda doesn't know. My eyes shut as I fought every image and every thought of *that* incident. In that moment I knew that my life was doomed. I knew that it really was over and that Amanda was *just* there for her own amusement. I let go of myself; I let it all just happen.

Weakness—there's nothing quite like it.

Back to my window: I just stood there awaiting mother to bring dinner. I stood there awaiting Amanda. You know in the movies when the character is waiting for their lover or friend and then they slowly melt in sorrow as they realize their lover is dead? That they won't ever come back? That's how I felt—only Amanda wasn't dead. Well I hoped not. At times I'd spend the whole day famished; just waiting. Or at times I'd shove something in the microwave—that's it. I couldn't really cook. I never learned how. I never wanted to learn how. I assumed that everything would be done for me—everything except for making friends. That's my responsibility and I let myself down. Amanda?

When I was a child they used to say, "Beverley is blind. Beverley can't see. Now Beverley don't you wish you *looked* like me?" Those were enough words to murder a child, let alone seclude a child, from all humanity. Those words threatened my life—I had to getaway. No one understood me. No one seemed to care. I was the blind girl who sat in the corner; who ate alone and who *was not special*. Being the joke and carrying a dunce hat on my head was my daily routine. I wished I could *see their faces* just to know if I *really* differed. Maybe they had vulgar bone structures or they were obese. I needed to know. I wanted to see Amanda too. I was a conformist. Her voice led me everywhere—I needed to know *what* she was.

After a while of thinking and drowning in thoughts I left to *the park*. Where everything was alright. I walked around and inhaled the air—maybe Amanda will be here. All I wanted to do was inhale the air. "You should've seen her Louis Vuitton. Simply amazing." a girl said as she walked passed me. "Completely fabulous. I must get daddy's card." the other girl replied. I then felt jealousy— where was *my* daddy? I didn't have a card to buy Louis Vuitton. I borrowed mother's every designer possession— sort of borrowed. Mother was afraid that someone would steal my designer item—ridiculous-ness. Her things weren't 'anti theft' either, she thought. I could take care of myself though—or so I believed.

And then I bit my lip as thoughts of the delivery boy wandered my mind. What *was* his name? Did I really kiss a boy? My eyes remained shut as I reminisced on something that happened recently. Hours ago, 'recently.' I'll just stay there for a while. I liked that feeling. I'll just remain here until it's over. Until I'd have to hunger for more. I hungered for more.

Brian—was his name. A fiery intensity of feeling suddenly quaked my body. I never felt *that* before. I longed for him. Right now. I actually *wanted* a boy and I knew that he would *want me again*. It's happening to me—the way I want it to be—finally.

It began...

"What are you so jolly about?" "Oh Amanda! I've missed you." "I'm certain. So, spill." I couldn't control my smile. I was—happy. "Brian." I said. "Ha! The pizza boy?" I paused and then whispered, "I want him *sexually*." she suddenly laughed and I was clearly a fool—or not. "Well... I don't have the key to your *thingy*." she said. "Shall I do IT?" I whispered. "If you really want to—" "No, do *you* think I should?" she then paused. "Yes. If *you want* we can order another pizza—" I then interrupted out of excitement. "And then he'll come!" "Yes, he shall." "You're the *best* thing that has ever happened to me, Amanda." "Ditto *darling*."

I couldn't wait to return home. All I thought about was Brian. His cologne, his lips; the sex. 'Beverley, where were you?" my mother asked as her back pressed on the kitchen counter. "At the park. I was—*bored*." Surely I was. I knew then that even if I were to order pizza and even if Brian delivered it, there was no way in hell that mother would accept him. She would call him a 'gold-digger.' That was probably her technique to prevent boys from hurting me, but not this one. Not Brian. I had a plan. "You must be famished." Mother said. "Oh no, I've eaten—something." Amanda stood beside me and mother *couldn't* care to greet her. Maybe she was drunk, as usual. It *was* night-time anyway. "Aren't you going out tonight, again?" I asked as she poured a drink into her glass. She only drank champagne at that hour. "Do you have plans, Bev?" "I was only asking because, well, Fred was here with his girlfriend and—" "Oh don't remind me of her. Please." I just stood there awaiting an answer.

"But no. I'll be home tonight. I'm expecting a—visitor." mother shyly said. Damn it. Brian, I thought... "Beverley, there's always tomorrow." Amanda whispered. "I guess so." "Pardon?" mother said. "Nothing. I wasn't talking to *you*. I knew the night would end quickly and Brian wouldn't be here. It's not like he knew how I felt. But he must have felt the same sensation—or so I thought. "Let's go to your room. Discussion time."

Amanda walked into my room as though she owned it and jumped on my bed. "So, what's the plan?" "Well nothing *can* be done today. Maybe tomorrow." "Oh don't be silly. We'll ring Pizza Hut and demand to speak to Brian. I'll remind him of *whom* we are." I gave her my phone, my sad old fashioned phone. Mother denied buying me something new. I was surprised that Amanda memorized the number—so quick. "Hello. I'd like to speak to Brian please." she said while clicking her fingers at me. "Yes, Brian. Remember me? Truth or dare girl. Yes, what's *your* number?" I just stood there in amazement. "Why not? Oh come on. Well because I have a surprise for you." she continued. Amanda had guts that I wish I had. She really was a star that one. "Alright, great. Then we'll see you tomorrow. 12pm. Cheers." Unbelievable. "Alright, so he wouldn't give his number, *but* he'll come over tomorrow—on his day off." I felt a sudden spasm throughout my body. "Serious?" I shrieked. "So what will you wear? We need to sort-*this*-out." she mumbled as she twirled me around. "You're fortunate to have a friend like me." And I was indeed.

Whatever outfit she chose didn't really matter. I knew that I'd look great—somehow. "So you really want to do this?" Amanda asked as she played with my hair. "Yes." "You know, if you drink, it might make things less complex." "I don't drink and I don't smoke." I said. "You should. Your social life will be tremendously social—like." I knew it was wrong, I couldn't smoke and nor could I drink. "Just a sip? I saw the alcohol in the kitchen." "My mother drinks and so does Frederick." "See? Everybody does it. So should *you*!" "I'll die." "We'll all die—eventually. Just *live your life* will you?" "If my mother finds me wit—" "oh she won't. I'm here for you." Amanda convinced me into doing something dreadful— something I wanted but feared trying. "You stay here." I snuck my way to the kitchen and carefully looked over my shoulders. I had to be certain that it was safe. I could hear mother speaking—on the phone. 'Just do it.' a voice in my head echoed. I quickly grabbed the bottle of champagne from the table and ran upstairs. Surprisingly enough mother heard nothing. "Good girl. Bring it here!" "Oh the glasses." Forget them." She said. We spent the night sipping from the bottle and sharing stories. I spoke most of the time. Amanda was attached to the bottle. "See how good it feels?" I nodded in response although I didn't quite understand her. "This—this is how it's meant to be."

"What's the first thing you'll tell Brian?" I reached for the bottle and tilted my head back as I drank. Have

I done this before? "I'll say hello and goodbye." I said as my head spun. "Silly girl. Say you like him—say you want him. Desperately." Desperately? I wasn't desperate although I *did* want him. "And then?" she pulled me close and demonstrated what had to be done. She gave me the deepest kiss I've *ever* felt. "Do that." I bit on my lip before I took another sip. "That was nice." "Exactly. You want *him* to say that—understand?" "Uhuh." I replied as I licked the very top of the bottle. "Oh and you might do *that* to his *thing*." "Do *what*?" I yelled as I moved back. "You know. Lick and suck on his—ding dong. It's fun; trust me." She went too far. I wouldn't do that—at least I thought so. "Well that's part of it. You'll do *that* and he'll do *this*—" she said as she reached for my jeans. "*What* the bloody hell *are you doing?*" I asked as I separated my jeans from her hand. "Practice makes perfect. You don't want him to runaway—now do you?" I shook my head as I curled up my toes. I was nervous and not so ready. I had an idea of what her intentions were and I did have self-control. But where was it? "Oh just trust me already." she said as she tugged on my zipper.

"Beverley darling; are you asleep?" mother yelled. "Someone wants to greet you." she continued. "I'm busy with—something." I replied. I assumed her 'guest' was here; probably the man who visits her with that expensive car, and cocky accent. You know *those* ones. Before I could yell that I'll be down in a minute, Amanda's mouth loitered on my femininity. Her *mouth* was right down there. I couldn't stop her—I didn't want to. I shut my eyes and accepted the moment. All I could do was moan.

She was good—so good to me. "You like?" she asked as I held my breath. "Yes." I gasped. I didn't want her to stop. I wish she didn't. She just went deeper and deeper until she was over. I just stood there; my knees shook. What was next? Amanda then stood up and kissed me. She pushed me on the bed and began to squeeze me.

Before I could return the favor I heard:

"Stop crying you little tart. You deserve this. You know you like it. No one else will do this to you—not my way. Enjoy it."

Those words I shan't forget. They haunted me—and forever will. "What's wrong?" Amanda asked as I pushed her to the side. "Nothing. You need to go." "Are you sure?" "Yes, Im just tired." "Alright then. I'll see you tomorrow. Your dress is on the chair; don't forget." "I shan't." I laid there on my bed as Amanda climbed out the window. Was that how it was meant to be? Who am I?

I woke up the next morning without a drop of regret. But what really happened last night? I stared around as though I expected Amanda next to me. I touched my lips and then lowered my hand—all the way down. All I could feel was Amanda. Her scent was everywhere. What has she done to me? I felt something real. I laid on my bed thinking if summer could ever get any better. Then suddenly it hit me: I've changed. Before I met Amanda I never would have thought about kissing a girl. I never would've—kissed a boy. The taste of alcohol—that of which I never would've tasted. My life had only just begun and all because of one person: Amanda. What *w*as her surname? I shant ask. She'll just be *Amanda*. The idea of being with Brian kept me nervous. I was afraid. He could be vigorous—or gentle. I had to find out.

After taking a steamy shower I rushed downstairs and grabbed a slice of banana. I didn't want Brian to see a bloated belly. On top of that, *they* were probably on their way here. I continued to wait as I scribbled on paper. "Here I am!" Amanda yelled. I jumped in excitement and ran to the door. "You're not wearing your dress." "I know. I didn't want to make it dirty." "Well he *will* be here soon. Go change." Of course she helped with the makeup and hair. I would've said I looked captivating, but yeah... "Beautiful." Amanda whispered in my ear. "Thank you." "So, you know what to do? I won't be here for long." "Why not? Please stay." "I can't stay while you're have fun—unless." she paused and continued. "oh never mind, I'll watch a movie downstairs." "Alright." "Wait! One other thing; the perfume." "Right." The doorbell rang. My heart beat was uncontrollably fast. "Don't worry. This ought to be interesting." On our way downstairs Amanda whispered, "remember that size *does* matter." Whatever she meant.

As soon as the door opened I heard, "Oh wow. You look—ravishing." Just what I needed to hear. "These are for you." Brian said. "Oh I'll take them." Amanda said.

"Sit down, please." I said as I pointed at the sofa. "So, what's it like to be blind?" Not the smartest question ever. But it worked. "It *can* get boring. Not seeing colors and all, you know." "I reckon you see blurs of some sort?" he asked. "No." was he here just to question my blindness? "Well, I still think it's fascinating." he said as I smiled. "How old are you?" "Twenty-one." I then paused and pulled myself away. "Am I too old?" he asked. "Of course *not!*" Amanda said. "Right, Bev?" she continued. "Uhuh." "So did you mean what you said, on the phone?" he asked while touching my hair. "Well—of course." "I—I want you too." he stuttered. I bit my lip and pointed upstairs. "What?" he asked. "My bedroom." "Do you want some *champagne*, Brian?" Amanda asked. "Surely I do." "Beverley?" "Ha-ha. No no. Not for me." I replied before Amanda cleared her throat ever so loudly. I knew what *that* meant. "Of course I want champagne, Amanda." I quickly said.

"So, Beverley. You live with your parents?" "With my mother." "Sibling or something?" "Well, a brother but he's around your age." He then laughed. "What's funny?" "Well, I bet your brother would kill me." Frederick probably would've killed him and then buried him as well as spat on his grave. "Don't be silly." I shyly answered. We seemed to be getting along—I liked it. "One for you—*you* and I." Amanda said as she handed us our drinks.

After an hour, or so, of laughter and jokes, Brian asked to see my room. Amanda remained downstairs of course. He fancied my room and thought that it was spacious. "So have other boys entered *this* chamber?" he teased. "Not quite." "I see." he said as he paused. "Has any other boy touched *this*." I spasmed as his hand brushed against my breast. "Not quite." I replied. He then moved closer and his cologne was gratifying, it was something musky with a hint of sweetness. I then felt his lip on my neck—honestly thought he planned on biting me; but no, he wasn't a vamp. His lips slowly graced my neck, and against my instinct, I swiftly yet passionately returned the favor. I followed his every move—almost. "I like your dress." he whispered as he nibbled on my ear and then slowly, but surely, removed my dress and began to brush his lips on my body. *It's no wonder that Amanda did what she had done last night, to me.* Brian then grabbed me and twirled my body as though I weighed a feather, and then tossed me on the bed—even though I was oblivious to where I was landing.

Brian reminded me that I was beautiful and sexy, he slowly kissed my knees and then my inner thighs again. "Brian." I shyly said as he whispered my name, almost as though to tease me—with a hint of seriosity. His lips kissed the tip of my femininity (that's what I call it and I refuse to say 'vagina.' There, I just said it.) He then whirled his tongue like a tornado as both my legs extended in opposite directions—my moans wouldn't stop him. It was as though I asked for more; when I said nothing at all. As he began to kiss my lips I felt a sudden penetration, and then pulled him deeper as his name departed my mouth. He quickly tossed me around; right on all fours. My face—opposite the window.

He suddenly laid on his back and said, "it's your turn baby." My turn? What must I do? I just sat there and stared into darkness. "My turn?" He grabbed my lower back; almost touching the peak of my *cheeks* and then he began to slowly move me into circles. "Oh I get it." I slowly said as I enjoyed the feeling and removed his hands as I continued on my own. I'd rather do things like that than be a complete and utter loner—at least I felt alive, but there's still more to it than just *this*. Brian quickly tossed me over and said, "I've got this." After our fiery experience, we laid there panting as though we hiked Mt. Everest. And although I was covered in his sweat, I didn't mind laying there beside him. His hand rested on my stomach as he said: "I needed *that*." And my sigh was an adequate reason for him to believe that my feelings were comparable to his.

That night was completely irreplaceable.

Brian and I spoke for a while before he left.

Amanda attacked me with various questions—she needed to know everything. I just sat there and explained what happened. I've never heard of someone *this* excited about sex. Lol. "More champagne?" I shook my head. I drank enough for this week. "How was it?" "Marvelous." "*Just?*" Perhaps she wanted me to make use of every word in the dictionary. "Yes." I do plan on seeing him again. "You want him again; don't you?" I nodded. "Why you naughty little bitch." "Aren't *you* the bitch who taught me?" I've never used such vulgar diction in my life. Amanda has turned me into a wild-ish creature. And I liked it. "And you enjoyed it." She sighed.

"You learn quickly...Isn't it?" she asked. "I reckon..." "No, you do. I could use you sometime." Use me for what? She must be drunk. "What?" I asked. "Nothing." I sensed the awkwardness but it was inevitable. "We should go out sometime, soon. There's so much you need to see—do. On top of that, so many guys are out there. For you. All for you." Everything happened so fast; I began to wonder whether it could change if I gained sight of things. If it was possible. Maybe Amanda *is really here* for a reason. Maybe she's here to teach me something—a reason to live. "When I feel low, I just listen to John Mayer. He helps." "I know. So do I. Sometimes he's all I have." For a moment I felt quite shallow but at least someone else shared shallowness with me. "There's no point in taking this temporary life ever so seriously. The rope is bound to cut. We'll all be gone soon—*even yourself.*" I hated the idea of death but the whole concept of life alone was saddening. It will all be gone soon—Amanda was right. It's all just temporary.

"Have you ever loved someone?" I asked Amanda as my hand quickly clutched my mouth. "Never." "Ever?" "Never ever." Her point was clear. But I failed to understand her emptiness. *Where was she from and who was she* for her to never have loved—someone?

Silence. It was as though loneliness conquered the earth. Silence. That simple question was all it took to tape her mouth. Amanda was mute. For now. "Don't ever believe someone who says they love you. No one ever loves—we just want. Need. We feed on others loneliness and replace our thirst with *compassion*—pretence. It's all a game, Bev. Don't ever fall on the contrary. It used to be that everything was about happiness. About family and friends. We ate what we were fed and we went where directed. But now—people can't seem to separate illusion from reality. There's always a shield set up for defense. Love. It's only an excuse to camouflage what truly lies between an enemy and a friend."

I stood there knowing that we're entitled to our own perspectives. But I couldn't tell her. I swallowed my pride—out of respect for anothers perception of life. "Just believe me—I know what's right." she said. You see, if I were a Samantha or a Betty I would've known that Amanda was wrong. If I were *just* someone else I would speak my mind—always. But I'm Beverley Whatman. I'm scared of the truth and I'm scared of losing a friend. The only friend that I have.

"But don't change who you are for what you think they will like."

"Let's go out." "I can't. What will mother say?" "Mother will say nothing. It's your life—remember?" I then inhaled *this* insidious air ever so deeply before I could oppose. "Yes." "She wouldn't have to know. Just lie." she then grabbed my wrist and said, "Lovely bracelet. Your mothers?" "Yes. It's from Tiffany's." "Even better." Amanda muttered. "Where are we going?" And *why* was she rushing? "Wait and see?" My hand was faithfully held by Amanda's as we walked away and further away from my home. I didn't know where we were. I didn't ask. I heard sounds of cars and people talking. The smell of cigarettes nearly choked my lung. A bar—she took me to a bloody bar. "Timmy, two cocktails please...*AND Tequila*." "Amanda. One is enough for me." "Oh Beverley darling, *live. Just live will you?*" We drank, but thoughts of mother never left my mind. Would she hit me? What would happen if she knew I was out— this late? I tilted my head back as alcohol rushed through my system. My innocent system. "Alright, can we go?" "Hello, it's summer time, Bev." "Please?" She then sighed as though she were assigned a difficult task. "Alright! Timmy, see you later—or something." I couldn't believe that we were leaving. Finally.

"Hold on *tight* to your belongings—we're taking the alias." Alias? What was wrong with the other way? "Uhhh—okay." I hesitantly replied. "If I were *you* I'd just whisper until it's safe." Safe? We continued to walk, without disruption; or so I thought. "Give me your wallet." I heard someone mutter. "No we won't." Amanda barked. I then heard a bottle bash against something. "Give me it—now!" the stranger threatened. "Bev, stand back." Amanda whispered as she pushed me. "We don't have money." "Give me *that* bracelet." Ultimatums should never be so complex. If I were to hand it over, I'd have to hand over my life. My mother would murder me—this is *hers*. "The bracelet—tart." "That wasn't quite necessary." I said. "I'll tell you what—hand me the fuckin' bracelet and I'll quit with the *unnecessary*." He said. I couldn't believe we carried a conversation, a debate actually—over *my* mother's possession, with some stranger. "Beverley, do it." "*Don't say my name*." I hesitantly muttered; as though it would *really* make a difference. I slowly removed the bracelet and held it hostage. I could smell the intruders desperation in wanting my bracelet. He needed money and he would kill for it.

"Excuse me." As soon as I heard someone else's voice, other than Amanda's and the intruder's, I felt a spasm throughout my body. This was *it*! *We're rescued. "Excuse me.* Do you have spare change?" Didn't this man see that we were being ambushed? Or was he blind too? Deaf—maybe! "This creature is stealing from us." Amanda quickly confided. Before I could utter a word something snatched the bracelet *off* of my hand. Just like that. *They* were both gone—together. We *were* completely and utterly *ambushed*. "Fuck fuck fuck!" Amanda repeated. "Fuck!" I yelled. "I can't go home. Can I spend the night?" I continued. "That's not possible. My parents—I'm staying with my aunty right now. She doesn't support the idea of sleep-overs." Amanda said. I knew that I had to lie to mother—yet another lie.

My arrival was expected; my presence was not—I could sense it. I only heard a cough before I quickly jumped out of fear. "Is *this* what you are now? The girl who creeps out in the night and returns at dawn?" It wasn't dawn but I understood her quite well. "Sorry mother. I—I feel asleep on the bench, in the park. I realized how late it was and so I rushed home. Swiftly." "So you drink now? I can smell the alc. from *here*." She said. "It wasn't me. Maybe someone in the park poured a pint on me." I then paused and said something stupid—out of the ordinary really. "Maybe when it rained it smelled like alcohol, somehow?" Stupid. "Maybe. And maybe *that Jane Norman* dress just fell from the sky. And Maybe my Champagne bottle drank itself. And maybe my bag just took itself outside for a stroll that day?" she said. There I stood, caught in a trap that I built on my own. "I understand that being alone, not having friends, can be tough. I know that *darling*. But don't change who you are for what *you think they* will like." she muttered. "I'm not. I haven't done anything wrong." "Then explain the whereabouts of my bracelet—the Tiffany one." Silence. I had an answer but I wasn't ready to reveal it to her. "I don't know." "Now you want to blame Frederick?" Absurd. I didn't bring up

Frederick—she did. Maybe *she* never trusted him. "It could be. You don't know Frederick." I said. "But *you* do?" I figured that maybe, arguing about Frederick would change her perspective, and save me. But it won't happen. We stood there arguing about the truth. Frederick was and will always be superior to me.

"Go to your room. Now." was, sadly, the only thing she could say after realizing the truth. It wasn't the fact that I've changed—I'm changing. It was because I wasn't Frederick. I wasn't normal and popular. Nobody dated me and nor did they want to. Mother was afraid that I'd wind up lonelier and vicious—miserable and that maybe she would need to accompany my misery. She couldn't handle that fact because she had a life. A life that I'd never have.

There I was, lonely again; standing by my window. Almost as though I could see everything in front of me. Everything that I wish I could see. I thought about my life—well now that I actually have some sort of life, but was it worth living? I'm glad that I've got a friend like Amanda—but is *that* enough? Is that all that we need to truly survive in this world? I was uncertain. But for a second I managed to convince myself to hold on. Just for a while. There's always a lie behind the truth; so I guess I'll just wait and see what happens. I never really thought that these things would happen to me. Stealing clothes; drinking alcohol; being robbed and kissing a bloke. I never thought for one second that *that* would be me. Here I am; a liar and a fake. At least I'm somebody now. Have you ever wondered about tomorrow? You know; whether tomorrow will add something extremely beneficial to your life? Well I always wonder. Always.

I thought about Brian for a quick second—I didn't love him. I only wanted him. Did he love me? *Could* he love me? Me—the girl who can't see. I might as well not feel anything and have nothing felt for me. That's what I deserved—well is it what I deserve? Amanda. Where is she? I needed her now. She would know how to escape this moment. It's quite suicidal really—and it's ironic how mother thinks that staying here, in my bedroom, is safe. You're quite wrong, Mother.

"Beverley." I heard Amanda say as she knocked on my window. A smile suddenly grew upon my face. There she was. I quickly opened the window and let her climb in. "Do you *always* stand here?" "Maybe." I said. "Are you alright?" I stood there as I began to wonder, why the window? Why does *she* choose the window?" "I'm doing well—splendid actually." Liar.

"So, what's for your birthday?" I never told her my birth date—I never told anyone really. My family knows but it's predictable, of course. "How do you know?" "Well *you* told me about it?" Perhaps I did. "Well, it's very soon, and I haven't planned it. Yet." "I can do *that* for you if you want." I then sat on my bed and muttered, "nothing too big. Nothing big at all." "Well surely you want Brian there...right?" I nodded. "I'll tell you what—we'll go somewhere special. Alright?" she said as she caressed my cheek. "I'm here for you. Always." she continued.

Amanda and I sat there and spoke about the future and the past. All of the things that we've encountered—well, that *I've* encountered. We really weren't different; Amanda and I. We were sincere to one another and that's all I needed. Sincerity. And summer was quickly coming to an end but I wish it hadn't. Life has only *really* begun for me and I know that things would change when school starts again. I took Amanda's hand and said, "let's make a pact." "A pact?" "Yes. That we'll remain best-friends forever. *Forever.*" "Do you have a knife or a scissor?" I continued. "Well; I *do* carry this pocket knife with me now, *just in case.*" Before I could ask her to remove it from her pocket I felt a sudden prick. "Ouch!" "We shall suck on each other's blood to seal the pact. First, we shall say *it.*" She said. It seemed scarier than it was although this was quite my idea. "Best friends forever." "And ever." We then slowly sucked on each other's thumbs. Her blood was sweet—bittersweet. Ironically she thought the same about mine. "Wow—*that* was my first." I said. "Ditto."

I never thought that I'd do something like that. Suck on someone else's thumb—on their blood. It sounds rather vulgar—disappointing really. I sat on my bed and stared into my world. I could hear Amanda breathing and nevertheless she failed to question me of my actions. I figured that, for a moment, she would think I were insane. But then perhaps we're insane together? Of all the people I've met, Amanda was completely a rollercoaster. With her you have the ups and downs, and then the ups again with the back-flight and twist. And it seems as though you'll never drop once *you're up* again. "Now what?" Amanda questioned. "Now we wait until the blood flows through our *entire* system. Ha-ha!" My reply was rather "nervously" odd, but I really couldn't think of anything else to say. "What will you do once summer is over? It's almost there." I wish she never asked me that but I've questioned myself too. "I don't know, Amanda." "You'll be back at school; where the *normal* people are and then you would forget about me. I'm sure you'll make new friends." "I haven't quite made friends in that school; so why would it happen now?" she then grabbed my hand and whispered, "I just know it, Bev. Things will change." I was afraid—just a bit. Afraid of the fact that I'd befriend someone else. And then what? I'd have to start all over again; which I don't want. Where would *that* leave Amanda? "We just made a pact. It *will* stay that way." Amanda said.

Days passed by; and I was alone. Amanda was nowhere in sight. So much of a best-friend she was. My birthday is tomorrow but *where* was she? I couldn't stop thinking of how she said—"things will change." How could she be so certain? What *if* things change—and somehow I think they will. I'll just wait, or perhaps she's waiting for me by the park? *I'll just wait.* Mother also spoke to me about my birthday. Ironically she said, "you'll be 19 soon. Things *will* change." There it was again: *Change.* My birthday was only one day away and yet I felt normal. Neutral. Just the same as any other day. Things will not change.

Later on that day, I thought about Brian. I didn't know whether to call him or to wait. I've waited for too long—but I'll just wait some more. It's quite hard to live when you're living alone. Although I have people around me I still feel lonely. I should be used to it by now. I'm almost 19 and yet my life requires a sprinkle of more spice. Amanda taught me things, different things, and now I hunger for more. I'm just afraid that my wanting "more" will lead to a tragedy somehow. I should've stayed away, but I chose to remain. I chose to encounter all the bad that I could. "Darling, you *should* be excited. Why are you sitting *there* like that?" mother asked. I honestly thought she was at work. "It makes me feel something." "Oh, don't be ridiculous. Tomorrow is *the* day! Frederick and his friends will come." she yelled as she walked toward the kitchen. "Oh, there's food ontop of the counter; if you like." she continued. And just like that, she was gone. I was left alone…again?

"Wake-up sweet stuff! It's *your* sweet 19th b-day!" I heard Amanda mumble in my ear. Funny enough I didn't care for that moment. I awoke to a bitch of a migraine. Everything felt fuzzy and my eyes felt peculiar. Was I dreaming? I slowly shook my head and said, "Amanda. What is *that*?" "What's what?" I slowly tilted my head in absolute disbelief. I was dreaming. It really can't be. "What's wrong with you, Bev?" Was I the only one who noticed *this*. I slowly pulled myself up as I struggled to stop the pain in my head. "Are you alright?" I placed my hand in front of me, almost as though to touch Amanda's face. I started to move my fingers and then my wrist and my arm. I still failed to believe what was *right* in front of me. My lips quivered as I tried to find a reason—an explanation for *this*. "Amanda, do you see?" I then crawled out of *my* bed and headed toward the light. I walked to the window; my window. Was I dreaming? I turned around in amazement and asked Amanda if she could see me. "What's wrong with you?" "I-I—I can see!" I obviously stuttered as I touched the window and the ground. I kissed my hands and ran toward Amanda. Her eyes were green and her hair was long, brown and wavy. "Am I dreaming?" I asked as I began to cry. "Happy sweet 19." She whispered as she embraced me.

I quickly ran out of my room and then downstairs. "Mother!Mother!" I yelled. I then stopped right before the kitchen-counter; where she stood. Shocked. She was staring at me as though I were a zombie. Her hair was long and brown. She was tall and beautiful—absolutely beautiful. She was my mother. *My* mother.

"I knew that one day this would happen, *habibti*. I hoped and prayed." she said as she slowly walked toward me with open arms. I felt accepted— wanted. I felt significant and all of this happened because of a migraine? We spent hours laughing and touching each other's faces. It was almost as though we were—strangers to one another. We were. "You can see!" she yelled as she jumped for joy. We then began to cry together and for the first time in my life I witnessed and appreciated my own tears.

The hardest part was that school was beginning soon. What would *they* say? How would they look at me? For a minute I secluded thoughts of Amanda from my mind. I was ready to befriend other people. I was ready to see the world *as it was*. Frederick. I would have to face him—and then what? I'm not certain I can stand it. Would mother know? "Don't drown in your thoughts, darling." Amanda hissed. "Are *you* alright?" I mumbled. "Yes. Do I look unwell?" she asked as I shook my head. There was obviously something wrong *here*. "How does it feel—to finally see?" "Amazing!" I yelled as I swirled like a ballerina. She suddenly bit her lower lip. "Oh." she whispered. "So, like, how will it be *now*?" she continued. I stopped swirling and gazed at her with a confused facial gesture. "How? Now?" I slowly said. "Don't pretend, pretty little *Beverley*. Look at yourself! Just one day of sight-seeing and you *already* think you're a movie star." "What? I—" "Liar. And now you shall forget me? As though I meant nothing to you?" "Slow down. I haven't done anything wrong." "Yet." She said as she folded her arms. I felt extremely awkward and disrespected. What have I done to deserve this? All I did was gain sight and happiness. We stood there in complete silence—staring at one another and for once I could actually see her reaction. It felt good and yet so wrong. "Anyway, school starts soon and I guess you'll need time with your *new* friends, isn't it?" "What're you saying?" I asked as my head slowly began to feel rather heavy. "I'm *saying*—oh never mind. Just do your thing and I'll do mine. Your belated birthday gift is under your pillow." Before I could thank her she just disappeared. It was as though the air swallowed her—if that makes any sense.

I lifted my pillow and to my surprise my mother's Tiffany & Co. bracelet was right before me. "How?" I asked myself. A thief stole it a couple of nights back. How could it be *here*? How did she find it? *"How"* was the only word I could pick up at that very moment. It could've been from the shock or something. I knew that, somehow, I was saved and that somehow I was not.

I haven't seen Amanda since that awkward day. I could've said something wrong, or done wrong. I can't remember. Maybe she was right when she said I needed time alone—with new friends; an idea of which I grew quite certain of. "Are you hungry? I'll make you anything." mother said as she cleaned the kitchen. "No, I'm alright." "The family's coming tonight. They want to see *you*." she said. It felt as though they never wanted to 'see' me before. Was I such an embarrassment? "Have I ever told you just how *beautiful* you are?" I stood there as my lips began to quiver. Right then and there I knew that my life has changed. "You have." I said.

Four walls.

Still I heard nothing from Amanda. Has she forgotten about me? Here I was starting school; my final year and she's not here. Somehow she's a part of me and I can't seem to let her go. I don't want to. But for some reason I knew that I'd have to put her aside; just for now. I needed to make room in my life for new things. New people. New experiences. Amanda would be an obstacle. I couldn't believe I thought of her in that way; but it is what it is.

I needed to be with nature. Peace and quite—some alone time. *The park.* I knew the route and the sightings were breath-taking. Never have I seen such beauty— probably because I was blind before. As I walked to my destination I touched almost everything in sight. I inhaled the air and stared at the sky. I screamed inside of me—I was that happy. *This* is my place. This is where I belonged. I spent most of the afternoon at the park as I enjoyed the scent of the roses and the perfection of the trees and ground. Everything was perfection.

When I returned home I honestly believed that I'd meet Amanda. Naught. Nobody but myself. I then forced myself to believe that *it* was over—the friendship I once had was done with. It was time to restart. Such a sad feeling but I guess life is about surprises—even the bad ones.

I then laid in bed as I thought of tomorrow. Will they laugh as I walk down the hall? Will I find a boy as cute as Brian? Brian—where is he? Will the teachers continue to adore me as I thought they did? Maybe they just adored the *me* whom they sympathized with. I laid in bed that night like an insomniac creature. I wanted tomorrow so badly that my eyes refused to shut—my brain refused to rest. It was as if I were working for a cause. Excitement conquered me but just for a while.

The next morning everything felt new. It was as though I were a new person in a new world. Today—it's finally here! "Beverley." Mother said as she knocked on my door. "Yes mother it's time for school." I yelled in utter excitement. After a short but delightful shower I got dressed and ate breakfast. Mother always used to bring me to school and she promised that she would today. At least until I'm ready to go alone. "Alright pumpkin, we don't want to be late!" Suddenly I felt as though I were a child—it was a good feeling but bad at the same time. Would it change?

It was barely a fifteen minute drive to school. I saw other girls and boys wearing uniforms. Some were casually dressed. *Uniforms?* I quickly grabbed mother's hand and muttered, "*uniforms?*" "Oh you'll get used to it. Now be strong and enjoy your first day of your last year." Alright, she had a point there. But suddenly I felt afraid. I didn't *want* to go, but I needed to. As soon as I stepped on the school-ground my heart began to race. This was *it* for me.

I swallowed spit before I waved goodbye to mother. "I love you, habibti!" she yelled as she drove off. I was alone in a sea of school children just waiting to batter me. Waiting.

I had no choice but to walk—introduce myself or wait for someone to do it. I continued to stare at those who I thought were potential friends, and yes, I hoped they would step to me first. How odd. "I love your hair and bag." I quickly stopped staring and began to think, "are *they* talking to me?" *They* who looked as though they belonged in the glossy covers of Glamour magazine? I failed to believe that for just one second I'd make friends with perfection. I continued to stand there in complete awe. "I said—" she continued. "Samantha, we need to go." another girl said as *Samantha* quickly nodded. "What's your name?" "Beverley Whatman." "We'll see you later then." Have I already befriended them? *Already?* I was so desperate for that to occur again that I accepted anyone.

When I entered the school *they* were staring at me— most of them. They stood there as though I were VIP of some sort. They looked quite shocked, really. "Is that *really her*?" I heard some say. "She was blind—wasn't she?" Hello, I was right there and I could hear every blood thing you said. Of course I couldn't say *that* aloud. I was afraid to chase any 'potential' friend. And so I continued to walk—away.

It took a while for me to navigate my class. Entering it was quite a mission since people just stared. I wasn't an animal or something. Even teachers gazed at me rather strangely. "Welcome back, Beverley Whatman. Welcome back." Mr. Paterson said as he happily pointed to a seat. "Thank you." I couldn't bother turning around as I already knew all eyes were on me—such a special feeling but *freaky* at some point.

"So, what have we done for summer?" Mr. Paterson asked us.

Yes, what have we done indeed. I was hoping someone would confidently share their summer-experience before I did. "I traveled to Italy." "I stayed here with family and my mates." "*I got laser treatment for my eyes.*" Someone *sarcastically* said. I could've sworn that my heart stopped beating for a while. Who would say such a vulgar thing? "Enough—Robert." the teacher said as he noticed that that remark was quite evidently aimed at me. I slowly stood up and cleared my throat. "Something happened this summer—a miracle if you will. As you all know, I once was—" and then I suddenly stopped as the class continued to stare at me as though I were insane. "Blind." I continued. "I—am not anymore." "Yes, we can *see* that." Robert said. "One more remark, like that, and you'll find yourself outside." Mr. Paterson yelled. I was glad that someone verbally protected me. If Amanda were here I'm quite certain that she would've kicked Robert's teeth in.

"Yes, it's quite a miracle indeed, Beverley." Mr. Paterson said as others nodded.

The day flew by and I was glad. As I stood outside awaiting my mother; Samantha appeared out of nowhere.

"So, *you* were that blind chap? I knew that I've seen you somewhere—I just couldn't seem to grasp a hold of *where exactly?* But then it hit me that we once sat together. Just once." She said as I continued to stare at her mouth wondering if those were lies or the truth. Honestly, I was happy that she's speaking to me and not at me. Her gang soon joined her and it was like a meeting of some sort. "So, you're *her*?" they continued to say. Yes, I was her. I was her.

"For a second I thought you were new here." "Yes, me too." "Samantha; have you invited her?" one girl said. "Beverley, if you want, you can attend my birthday party tonight." Was that an invitation or what? "I'd love to." She suddenly grabbed my hand and wrote her digits right on my palm. She touched me. "Great! We'll see you then! Dress sextatic!" *Sextatic?* Goodness, how much have I missed?

It was Friday and it was safe to say that I was actually living life. I couldn't wait to tell mother about the day, and the invitation. What would I wear? For the first time I'd actually choose what to wear—a captivating black or purple dress. I couldn't wait. "Going somewhere?" mother asked as she stood by my door. "It was beautiful, mother. New friends and a party." she then smiled as she scratched her head—almost as though she were in disbelief. "Lovely. Lovely." she said. "Do you want me to—" "Oh no, mother. I think *they* will pick me up." "I see." "The present?" she asked. "I'll just give her fifty pounds in an envelope." "Alright." she then left as she had errands to run. As usual...

After hours of waiting and anticipating the night; Samantha finally arrived. They were here and *it was time*. I quickly grabbed my purse and swung the door wide open. The first thing I saw was Amanda; hiding behind a tree. It could've just been a figment of my imagination. Of that I was quite uncertain. "Hello sexy!" they yelled. Right then and there I felt—what I've never felt before: worthy of ones compliment.

We arrived at Samantha's home and it *was utterly beautiful*. It was one of those Three-story homes with large windows and glass walls. It was amazing really. Music was as loud as it probably could get and people were everywhere. *This was a party*. "Are you thirsty?" "No, I'm alright." I answered. Within minutes Samantha held a cocktail in her hand—I wanted one too. I couldn't help but stare at it while licking my lips. "What, do you want some or something?" she teased. "Oh, before I forget: happy birthday." I said as I handed over her gift. Funny enough I then held her glass as she reached for the envelope I brought; I took an innocent sip of what lead to a glass, and another glass, and another.

The night was long and filled with surprises. Who knew that parties were *this* wild? "Have you ever tried, you know, drugs?" Samantha asked as her head slowly wobbled left to right. "No." "Elliott *over there* has *some* coke left over. Perhaps you'd like to try?" I couldn't tell whether she was referring to Coca Cola or "Coke—Coke." she did say drugs after all. I couldn't do it. I shant. "Just one sniff; that's it. I promise it won't hurt or anything." I stood there staring at her like a child. I was in an ultimatum. I

wanted to go home. "Oh Beverly—come on now. *Live!*"
"Alright. Just once."

Never have I felt so shallow and amazing at the same time. Who knew that pleasure and pain could ever co-exist? The party soon came to an end and I was quite pleased. I actually left feeling like *somebody*; for once. Elliott drove me home that night and I was quite surprised that he hadn't tried anything peculiar. He was more of a drugged gentleman. Really. I was waiting for him to kiss me or, at least, ask me questions. Instead he drove and minded his own business. When we arrived at my home, he said, "you looked ravishing tonight."

Gentleman-like.

Out of the *expected*; Amanda awaited my presence. She was in *my* room as though it belonged to her. "Where have you been?" I asked. "Shhh, your mother is asleep." I then squinted while I tried to maintain focus. "Had a jolly time? Made new *friends*?" she said in a calm and slow manner. "Yes. I have actually." "I see. And how about me then? Where does *that* leave me? A summer-mate?" "No, Amanda! Why would you think that?" "You can't even balance yourself. Have you drunk a bottle and sniffed cocaine? *I can tell.*" I quickly stared at the ground in utter shame. "Where have you been?" I repeated. "Here. All the while you forgot about me." "I haven't." "Yeah? Then explain to me why you ignored me tonight?" So, *it was* her whom I saw by the tree. It was her. "You?" I walked toward her as I tried to embrace her. "No. I don't need it. You lied to me. Promised to be best friends forever. And now—look! *Just look at yourself.* Disgusting creature. Who are you?" she yelled.

I was at loss for words. All I could do was curl up in bed and shut my eyes. Pretend that this was a dream. Pretend that Amanda would come to her senses. But I knew that I've destroyed the best thing that I've ever had.

The next morning I remained in bed—sick. The roughness of last night knocked me over completely. Where was Amanda? I asked myself as I stared around. I could hear mother speaking on the phone. All I wanted was silence. I needed to contemplate on certain things. Things like last night and Amanda. What have I done now? We're all bound to make mistakes but I didn't think it would be *this* soon. My head never ached as much as today—did I deserve this? All I wanted to do was live. Make new acquaintances—just live.

"You know, it's probably because you think so much of yourself." "AMANDA!" I yelled as I held my chest in complete shock. "What are *you* doing *here*?" "You'd love for me to vanish—disappear, isn't it?" she asked. "No. I just thought you were gone. Home." "What happened to you? Was it the *incident* with Frederick that clustered your mind?" Incident? I haven't told her anything about *that*—ever. "Yes. Remember? Things became a bit hazy in your mind after that day; correct?" was this a test of some sort? Why was she doing this? "Which lead to stealing, lies, and now; befriending *people* like Samantha." She continued. "Listen. You don't know Samantha." "Quite right, but then neither do you." Alright, so it *was* jealousy. "I'm not *jealous* or anything but I'm only helping." Right then my head began to spin. I couldn't understand any of this. It felt wrong and complex. Why me? Life has only really just begun for me.

"Oh, and the drugs of course. You've become *just like them* now." I felt ashamed to even argue. I knew she was right, but why? You would think that Amanda understood my situation—but I'm wrong. Am I wrong? It's times like this that makes a person want to end it all.

"I'm not your enemy. *They* are." she continued.

School never really was the same again. All of a sudden *they* adored me. I was 'popular' and pretty. The weekends continued with parties and dining in expensive restaurants; meeting boys and trying *different* things. Samantha and I grew close and for a second, just a second, I forgot about Amanda. I slowly began to change—the way I dressed and my appearance altogether. I was brand new and somehow I loved it. Somewhere inside me I thought this was wrong but I ignored that feeling. I carried on being blinded by the *popular* life.

Amanda and I met every now and then, even though she seemed more distant each time. Even when Christmas and New Years arrived she kept telling me that I've changed—but I ignored that too. I thought that life was meant to be lived to its fullest; without regrets. Someone told me *that* once. Even though seeing Brian with another girl never really fazed me; somehow I still was hurt. But I just moved on completely. One day I had an awkward feeling—I didn't want to socialize with Samantha and the rest of those people. Something was wrong. I knew it but I chose to seclude it from my mind...

Yet again.

One weekend, Elliott invited me to *his* party. The excitement couldn't be described in words alone. I really wanted to go—it was much anticipated. Much. As I stood by the mirror watching myself and thinking of my outfit, I then began to wonder: If it weren't for Amanda; would I still have all this? Who and what I am right now is because Amanda taught me. I can't pretend as though she meant nothing to me. Yes, there are days when I forget about her but is that my fault? Was I bound to only have one friend? Amanda. Here I am—a new person. A new life. New friends. A new beginning with Amanda in it—so it's not quite *new* if you will. Shall I go to Elliott or must I await Amanda's presence?

I chose to go. A mistake that I constantly regret. It also seemed as though Mother became busier and less compassionate towards me. Was it because I gained sight of things? Wasn't I like a lost and abandoned child before? "Amanda!" I heard them shout from outside. I quickly muttered, "I'm coming," as though they could hear me.

"Just go." I heard Amanda's voice mumble in my ear. I quickly pouted my lips one last time and rushed downstairs. "Sexy beauty!" Samantha yelled as she stood there with her knee-high boots and skintight jeans. She looked good. *"Are you ready for tonight?"* Elliott yelled. "Yes. Haha." "We'll just need to pick-up Meleny and Robert."

As we drove away singing songs and yelling out the window; I felt happy again. I liked that feeling and I wanted to keep it. It's usually Amanda who changes things—she makes me depressed somehow. Do I need her?

"Move over, over. Here they come." There we were. The five of us again. Living life as it should be—at least that's what I thought. "Pass it back here." Robert yelled. "Pass what?" I asked. There it was again; the white substance that seems to blind most of us. "Don't pretend you didn't enjoy that night." Elliott said as he quickly turned around, temporarily. "Here. You can use this table-thing," Meleny said as she pulled down the 'table-thing' that was behind the chair.

"Pigs!" Samantha yelled. "Excuse me?" "The cops are behind us! Alright, *we* are screwed." "Relax. They're not coming for us." Before we knew it, we had to pull over. That was it. It was over. We thought...

"You know you were driving too fast, don't you?" "Yes sir." "Out! All of you."

"We're fucked." Samantha and Melany muttered. "*How old are you lot?*" He asked. "Eigh—nineteen." "Not sure are we?" he said as he leaned over and dusted my shirt. My black shirt. Bollocks! "Coke—children?" "No. I was eating—a doughnut." I said as Samantha shook her head. "*T*his doesn't resemble a doughnut." the other pig said as he swayed the bag of cocaine; left to right.

"It's mine. Not theirs!" I quickly yelled *without thinking*, yet once again. "Oh, is it?" Samantha then nodded. Did she *really just nod?* "Let them go. Take me. It's all my fault really." I insanely continued. "The four of you," he said as he pointed at my *friends*, "the four of *you* will receive a warning and we'll notify your parents. *You* on the other hand, are coming with us. Understand?" I then quickly nodded.

Betrayal. There's nothing quite like it.

Four walls. I sat there as I was surrounded by four walls. It happened to me. I was one of those who received punishment—four walled punishment. Sitting in a cell where all I could do was contemplate on yesterday and tomorrow. The yelling and screaming scared me a bit—just a bit. I expected all of this. It's jail. I slowly curled up in the corner as I held back the tears that I've held for so long. "Don't think too much. Mother is on her way." I heard Amanda whisper in my ear. I was afraid but I knew this wouldn't last forever. My mind slowly eased as I carefully fell asleep.

"Beverley! Beverley!" I heard my mother yell. Was she really here? I slowly opened my eyes and there she was—in tears, but not quite. She seemed depressed and angry. Angry at me. "What have you done to yourself? Your wrist?" she then began to cry. I felt wronged but it was too late—I was already in here. "Get her out!" she yelled. Before I knew it; the door was opened and I was free? At last. After just one day of punishment. "I never should've *prayed* so hard." mother whispered in my ear as she embraced me.

"Mother, I—" "No. No explanations—please." I then just pushed myself back on the chair and watched as she drove us away. This was not the end. I knew there was more to come—and somehow I felt prepared. If that was the consequence then I was willing to face it. I chose to… "Everything will be alright. I promise. Everything will be alright." mother continued to mumble as her head bobbed back and forth.

"No. This is just the beginning—I fear for you." Amanda's voice whispered.

Being at school felt the same; except for the fact that *they* showed more respect. It was almost as though I were a heroine of some sort, the irony in *that*. I could almost see them clap for me as I entered the chambers of education. "Thank you, Beverly." Samantha said as she hugged me ever so tightly. "You're welcome?" "Why would you do that for us?"

"Because we're friends. What I did for you; you would do for me. Right?" she then uncertainly nodded. All I really wanted was to go home. I couldn't face the fact—this fact. I was not a heroine nor will I ever be. I just made a choice—a stupid and blind choice. It didn't take long for school to end. It was time to be alone and I couldn't wait. I imagined the things that Amanda would say—would she blame me or would I also be a heroine to her? Amanda saw things differently—that's the thing about it. The thing that I appreciate really. She wasn't quite like you and her—she was spectacular. But spectacular seemed to go by unnoticed.

I didn't bother remaining by the school-ground after class; I just went home. Loneliness was what I desperately needed, and somehow Amanda's presence seemed to have qualified. "I know you need me." Amanda said as she stood by my door. "I do. Tell me what I need to do—anything. Look at what I've done to myself!"

"I know. Such a desperate child. Such desperate measures and such a desperate definition of friendship." Right then and there Amanda seemed more mature than ever. Everything she said was correct. I was so desperate to define friendship that I chose to deface myself because of it. "I'm here now. I've always been. You've just never really noticed." she whispered.

"Tell me what to do. Anything—and I'll do it." I knew that Amanda was the only friend I had. The only choice and reason to live another day. The choice I made that changed everything...Amanda.

*"Frederick. Did you love me that day
when you hated me the most?"*

"Do it. He doesn't deserve to live. Do it." Amanda repeated as I stood above Frederick with a steel rod. How did this happen? What happened? *"Beverley, I'm sorry. I'm so sorry. Please!"* he pleaded. *"What you did to me was unjustified—and it will never be just."* I whispered as I raised the steel rod above my head. Was this it? Murder. Was it the only way out of this nightmare?

Amanda knew what Frederick had done to me. She knew that he had taken me for granted when I was blind, a blind child. It was a stupid choice that he made—but he did it. He thought that I embarrassed him by being blind. What I never understood was how a brother would do something so evil; dark and unforgivable to his blind sister—a person who is so vulnerable and innocent. I didn't deserve what happened to me. It's a nightmare I can never escape and nothing can ever make me forget.

Frederick's birthday was just two months before mine. He always spent it with us. This time he and I were alone—was it a coincidence? Or was it fate? As usual he would watch a movie and then his friends would join later. There was no 'later' this time. Amanda saw to it. "You can't let him celebrate while you suffer everyday." Amanda repeated as she banged her hand on the wall. "You can't. And you won't. I won't let you!"

"Listen to me now. Frederick deserves to burn in hell. You hear me?" I stood there while thinking about her words. She was right. Why must I suffer for something I didn't do? "Take this." Amanda said as she handed over a steel rod. "No. Amanda. No. Not like *this*." "How else? This is the only chance you've got. End it now. I'll forever be here. Your friend...always." she said as I smiled and naively grabbed the rod.

"Forever." she repeated.

There I stood above Frederick. I could feel the emptiness within him just by staring at him. He's so sorry now, isn't he? Look at him. You could almost sympathize along with him. Watch him as he shall plea for mercy. "Beverley. Think about mother. Think about yourself. You have so much going on now. Don't do this please. I—I love you." I then slowly tilted my head and asked him, "Frederick. Did you *love* me that day when you hated me the most?"

"He did not, Beverley. DO IT!" Amanda yelled. My arms slowly felt weak as I swung the rod towards Frederick—my brother. To think that today was his last really did scare me. As the rod hit his head all I felt was relief. Relief? It was almost over. "Again. Again!" Amanda repeated. I swung again, and again. I felt stronger each time—and I couldn't stop. What scared me the most was that I'm a murderer. I will remain a murderer until the day that I'm murdered. Even then, it wouldn't change...

"Write a letter. A suicidal one. This *must* look real." Amanda insisted. What's more real than death itself?

We shoved Frederick's body into his car and drove to *my* park. The park that I loved so much—I chose to hide him there. What an awkward choice. Frederick was pushed into the pond and then watched as he slowly disappeared. Was it over now? "Not yet." All I could do was follow Amanda's every direction. It was as if I were a soldier at war—I was there to kill. Just kill and somehow gain pride and honor. But this was my brother. What I've done to him can't be compared to what he did to me. We quickly drove back—not quite a distance anyway.

I've never scrubbed a floor the way I did that day. Blood was removed and it was almost as though Frederick never arrived here. "You know nothing." Amanda said. "Nothing." I said as I began to write *the* note. It was quite a short note actually. Quick and concise if you will. It was just hours before mother arrived. There she was with the cake and smile on her face. I continued to stare at her from my window—she hadn't noticed me, and neither did her friend. "Happy birthday to you! Frederick darling, where *are you!* Birthday boy?" she said as she continued to giggle with her manly friend. "He's probably shy." "Or dead." Amanda hissed.

Suddenly it was quiet. I walked downstairs as though nothing had happened. "Hello mother. Hello *William.*" "Where's Frederick?" "I don't know. I was asleep. Is he not in the bathroom?" "I checked. No one else is down here. Funny thing is, his car is right outside." Mother said. Fucking hell we forgot about the car. "I don't know. Call him." she then grabbed her phone and dialed. "He must be near-by. Or maybe he's with that tart." she joked as I smiled. "It's not working. *It's not ringing.*"

"Mother. What's this?" I said as I raised the letter I *found*. "It's from Frederick." I gasped. Before I read it aloud, tears already filled her eyes. It was almost as though mother knew what had happened. But she didn't really know. "What does it say?" she asked as I cleared my throat and adjusted my shoulders.

"Dear mother, as you read this I know you will hurt, and for that I'm sorry. I really wish things were different. You have Beverley now, you always have. Please forgive me. The only thing I regret not telling you is: I love you. I never meant to do this. Life is short, but mine was the shortest. It's better this way, really. You'll soon understand why I chose this road and I hope you'll find the strength to forgive me. I'm sorry... Love, Frederick." Mother continued to cry and yell as I read this note—our secret.

It was easy to see the pain in mother's eyes, but I couldn't show compassion. Not just then otherwise the secret would prevail. I was not ready for that...she wouldn't let me. As mother stood there, hoping that it was a prank, I had a phantom grin on my face...almost possessed. Frederick was gone and I knew the answer. The only answer that mother sought. Amanda stared at me as I grinned but she never questioned me. She always knew my every-move. She was like a conscience to me. Without her I'd be helpless really—a weakling.

Silence. The house never felt so empty before. Now that my mother constantly tried to figure out what happened to Frederick—it was as if I didn't matter. Nothing felt the same. Death just changed everything! They found Frederick's body floating on the water—it was bound to happen. They say some child was playing with a kite and then they found *that* corpse. What a nightmare it must've been...poor child. Other's asked why he did it and how. I just stood there in silence as I swallowed the answer each time. The guilt began to grow within me and Amanda wasn't there to help me. Where was she, yet once again? I was left to suffer on my own—for my own actions.

At school people stared at me as though I were strange, again. It was all happening *again* only this time I could see it. Silence followed me wherever I went. It was as though they knew—but they didn't *really know*. I was left alone *once more* because of fear. They all feared that I was a murderer—and because *I was*; I chose to seclude myself from them. Before I'd repeat it again.

Graduation was near, but I didn't feel like graduating. Everything felt wrong and slow. My whole life was set on pause and only I suffered. What have I done? Samantha looked at me differently. They all just did. It was almost disgusting and...just that.

I was disgusting.

I was alone. Loneliness never felt as cruel as it did that day. I was afraid to attend classes out of fear of being caught. *Maybe Amanda confided in someone who knew a person at my school.* I became more paranoid than ever—was this life? I needed to get-away. Everyday I would stare out of my window, as I did before, only to feel emptiness. Wrong. Un-human. I didn't belong here—not now and I'm not quite sure whether I ever *did belong*.

Whenever I'd stare at my mother she would look away—immediately. I could've sworn she knew. *Did she not love me anymore? What was the heart of the matter?* I'd only admit to myself that these were just rhetorical questions really—I felt like a fool. I did all of this and yet I expected someone else to take full blame—for something that I've done. Pathetic, isn't it? The things we do in life... for life.

Lost again. I stood in this world on my own—again. Yes I had family, but the friends I thought I'd always have have just disappeared. Just like that and I couldn't really question them—I'd only question myself and blame myself because I'm obviously the reason for all of this. For every consequence that I've planned for myself, without really knowing it, had made my suffering. I really wish things could change but then again who doesn't? I'm just Beverly Whatman and I think I've really lived up to my surname. "Whatman." Will I ever be somebody—or go places; meet different people and taste all there is to taste—out there? At times I'd just wish I was never born, never here. I feel as though I've put everybody through pain. Everything I know, or once knew has been defaced. Amanda—I really needed her now.

Even the park I loved was no longer there—for me. I was afraid to even think of walking there again. The only place where I could contemplate on things; the only reason I had for living. That park. It's gone now because of what happened to Frederick. I couldn't stand the blame. The fingers that point at me and people who whisper as I walk by. It's as though they knew—they were all blaming me already. I thought.

My mother spent more time at home and that only lead to more trouble. Arguments about who did what and where I've been. She would question who I was and why I was here. Why? Perhaps that's the consequence I must face, for what I've done.

The only place I could really find peace was in my room. Just being there, and even then thought's of what *they* thought of me just haunted me. What I anticipated the most now was graduation day. It would all be over and I wouldn't have to see those faces again. The more I waited the slower the days went by. Maybe it was because I was alone? I didn't know. I only assumed. Mother would cook but she hardly took time to really prepare a meal. At times I would order pizza and pray that Brian wouldn't deliver it. I could've turned to another pizza place but I guess I liked the feeling of not knowing whether Brian would come. Strange.

I'd find myself writing suicidal notes and then throwing them away. I'd do this everyday. Sometimes they were sweet, and other times they were *just* suicidal notes. I'd read them to myself and decide which one was *adequate*—but I guess none of them was enough seeing that I was still there, breathing. But the note that really worked my brain went something like this:

Mother. I love you! I swear that I do, and even though we've been distant I've always known and hoped that, someday, we would understand each other without questioning our differences. I just don't know when that day will come. I feel that, after Frederick's death things have gotten worse. Have they? I've only dreamt of being the daughter you never had. The one who was never blind, and lost; like I was—like I am now. Lost. Maybe when I find myself will I then be that daughter. Until that day, I will be gone. Please don't resent me after this. I love you. Your child, Beverley.

I even tossed *that* note away after I came to my senses.

Giving life another chance knowing that there wouldn't be *dramatical* changes—positive changes, and still hoping, was a plan that was bound to fail. That's what I thought. So, I just carried on pretending that everything would be alright. When Amanda visited me she knew something was wrong, but she didn't ask. I'd try to persuade her to ask me what was wrong with me. Did that make sense? She pretended as though everything was alright. I knew that nothing was alright and I wondered whether that's how it *always* was.

"Everything will be alright. I'm here." Amanda would *constantly* say. It felt good but it didn't really change anything. We still made Frederick disappear and that was not alright. My mother pretends as though I'm not here sometimes. That's not alright. It's definitely not *alright* that I've been having suicidal intents. *No.* Amanda couldn't see all of that. I just wanted her to know.

"Because I 'lived.'Just as Amanda told me to."

Graduation day. The day that I've anticipated just flew by. It was just another day, only I had a peculiar hat on my head, and a gown that covered my broken body. The most peculiar thing about all of this was my mother's absence. Amanda was there, but that wasn't enough. Mother didn't go because it would've reminded her of Frederick somehow. Was *that* an excuse? What kind of mother—well everything was my fault. Everything happens for a reason, and maybe it was time for me to really disappear. *Amanda would vanish with me, she would as long as I wanted her to.*

"I'm here for you. I hope you can see that now." Amanda whispered in my ear as tears ran down my cheek and dropped on my pink blouse. "I'm here for you too." I said as I wiped my forehead. It felt as though good things were yet to come and so I waited—impatiently. *This time* I didn't wait alone; Amanda was there. She promised that she wasn't going anywhere. We've been through so much to lose each other, really. I was there for her. She was here for me.

Nothing felt artificially sweet about *this*.

After days of not having a conversation of any sort with mother; she then yelled my name. She had something to say. I wasn't quite certain if I cared but somehow I found myself sitting opposite her—eye to eye. Listening to what *she had to say*. I cleared my throat as though I wanted to talk, *but no*, I just sat there. "*Beverley. It's quite clear isn't it*"

"What is, mother?" "This thing going on. Frederick's death affected the both of us, terribly. I can see that. We don't talk anymore. It's as if I live alone." She said as I continued to stare. "I just don't want things to continue this way. I don't want hatred—" "I don't hate you." I said. "You will. I'm afraid." She said as she wiped her tears. As I continued to stare at her, I cringed inside. How could I? I was the cause of all of this. I'm the reason for hatred, if there is any. Mother stopped talking and stared at me, almost as though she didn't know me. "You need change. You need to getaway for a while. I need to be alone. Peace." Peace? Was it not peaceful enough for her during the days we didn't speak?

"I love you. Right now I can't live with you. Just for now." She said. "What're you proposing—mother? Where do you want me to go?" I yelled as I began to shake out of fear of being alone, again and again. "It's only just for a while. I promise." "No, *where* are you taking me?" I yelled. "Your father agreed to—" "What?" I laughed. "Father? Who? The one somewhere in *Africa*? Is that it? You want me to go to Africa?" "See it as a mission. Finding your father." She said as she stood up. I didn't know what she meant by, 'finding' my father but I knew this 'mission' was obligatory. My life was like a movie at that point. "You're not joking?" I asked as she reached for an envelope on the table and said, "*this* is not a joke." while pointing at it.

There I was thinking that things would change for the better. Because I "lived." Just as Amanda told me to. I was wrong. Completely wrong. I wish I never gained sight of things. I should've remained blind. At least things would've remained the same. I stood up and ran to my bedroom—where I belonged.

"She *is* right, you know?" Amanda said as she spun in circles on my chair. "She needs peace and you need—something new." she continued. "I'm not going. I don't know who my father is, Amanda. Don't you understand?" "You don't even know whom you are. You need change. Get away for a while—away from all these prying eyes. People who force their way into business that's not theirs." She said. "No!" "If you don't go, you won't benefit much. Those suicidal notes will pile up, until one day, they will be read; while you're *gone*. Dead. Nothing but a memory. Is that what you want?" I couldn't answer. "But how about you? I'd be there without you." "Bev, I'm always with you. Remember?" I stared into her green eyes, as she stared into mine. I didn't want to accept the truth. "What if he hates me?" I muttered.

"Beverley. Do you hate yourself?" "No. But I've done things in this life—ugly things. You know it too! I don't deserve to even see my father. Why? So then I'd deface his life too?" I said while staring at the window." I will always be here. Your mother won't, and neither will your father. If you go, at least you'll know that you've tried to better yourself. Go. Get away!" she exclaimed.

If Amanda could accept it then I'd have to. Sometimes bad things happen so we can acknowledge the good and sometimes people do bad things for the sake of it. The things I've done have always lead to something—and this time I'm being lead to some place other than here. Is it worth it? Would I change? The fact is that: without Amanda, I never would've had *this* life. I would've been the girl with self-made artificial friends and constant vulgar intents of vengeance against Frederick.

I'm not. Anymore.

CHAPTER TWO

Bad habits die hard

I slowly and cautiously stepped out of the plane—to newness but not quite. My hopes were shattered…thank God! I was expecting lions and all sorts of wild animals awaiting my arrival. The first thing I saw was the sun, the beautiful sun as I walked down the stairway that was attached to the plane. As I slowly began to stare at the landscape I then squinted my sore eyes to embrace the beauty that I've never seen before. The air was new and the ground was hard.

"Beverley! Beverley is that you?" I heard my father yell—well at least I thought so. I slowly glanced at this man before I replied.

His lips were thick; his eyes were like fire and his skin—chocolate-like. It almost reminded me of the Toblerone I always loved back home. Was he really my father? He looked quite young—very young.

I don't know what or who *I* am. My eyes are green, my skin is olive-ish but my lips are also quite thick—he may have a chance after-all.

"Yes it's me!" I replied while wondering in uncertainty. "I've waited so long for this day. How was your flight? I hope they treated you well." he replied as he reached for my bags. "Oh no it's alright—I can carry them." I said. His arms were toned with a definite stature.

"Your father will not allow this. He gave me concrete orders." He said. "My father? So—you are not my father?" I asked. He giggled and never have I seen such perfection in teeth. He then said, "No. If I was, don't you think I would've embraced you already—and that I'd be older?" His accent was rather captivating in that I've never heard any like it before.

"I've heard a lot about you." he said as he carried my bags. "What's your name?" I asked. "Martin Boukrah." He replied. What a long and complicated name I joked to myself—I have friends with long names but just not like *this*. "What does Boukrah mean?" I asked Martin. "It means tomorrow."

"What is it that you've heard?" I slowly asked. "Well— let's enter the car first. You're father is awaiting you." As he passed by me his cologne was gratifying and it very much tickled my fancy. But I couldn't help but wonder if *that* really was the car he drove. "And that car belongs to *whom*?" I asked. "Your father—It's a beauty huh?" he replied. "Are you sure this is *his* car? What does he do?" I curiously replied. "Well—that's for you to find about, Madam Beverly." I blushed as he addressed me in such a remarkably formal way.

I never thought that I'd see a car like this here—yet ride in one even though we have a nice one in London. It was very luxurious and I wish I drove it. Who is my father? What if he owned a gazillion companies—better yet, what if he owned this country? Oh I forgot to mention again that my mother sent me to Sudan for two weeks along with three other significant destinations—all of which are part of my "1 year break." She believes that the man living here, or elsewhere, could be my father.

As the car drove away I was interrupted by the locals on the streets, the buildings and the language they spoke was quite innovative. "Is that Arabic?" I asked. "Aslan." he replied. I'm guessing that means "duh" in Arabic—or something equivalent. "What do you do here for fun?" I asked as my head constantly turned left to right in fear and amazement. "There are very many things to be done. We have the malls here, restaurants, Red Sea, The Nile, sandy deserts—can you believe they also have a Hilton Hotel here?" he said. Oh good, maybe that's where I'll stay. But judging from the car my father is likely to have a place of his own. Maybe a nice apartment put together—this car could be rented for all I know! "Are there any clubs?" I asked. "Of course. I enjoy going to the clubs every Saturday and Friday. We call Friday 'Youm-Al-Juma,' and we call Saturday 'Youm-Al-Sebit.'" He said. "Don't expect me to remember *that* anytime soon" I joked as I fixed my dress.

"How old are you?" he asked me with his hand twisted in the air, almost as if to exercise the wrist. "I'm nineteen—and a half. And you?" I replied with the same hand gesture while he laughed. "I'm too old for you!" Did I ask if he loved or wanted me—nope I didn't. "Seriously now—how old? "I'm twenty-seven." "Ooh you're so very old, Mr. Boukrah!" I joked. Well at least that was a good start—I hoped it would be that easy with my father.

"Where are we right now?" "We're in Khartoum." He answered. "Yes I know *that,* I meant which road is this?" "Shareh Amaraat." He replied as he turned the wheel to the right.

We suddenly came to a halt—we're here. "Are we there?" He made a 'tsk tsk' sound and said, "Why else would I stop the car by a gate? Are you supposed to be elsewhere?" he joked. Oh right, I guess he was absolutely correct. Needless to say that this was one giant gate—I wonder what could be behind it. Martin hooted and then a man around his thirties opened the gate. Maybe he's the guard for the complex? As he drove the car inside I was shocked by what caught my sight.

Are we in the right place? There, right in front of us stood a house—no, no a mansion. It was large with white paint on the walls and the ground was utterly immaculate. Before I could swallow my spit a couple of ladies—two actually, opened the house-door and came running toward me. I moved aback while they were singing—singing I said. They don't know me and yet they welcome me with such hospitality. "See? I'm not the only excited one to see you." Martin said. Yes I can see that, now I wonder where my father lingers. "Welcome Beverly—Welcome!" they said as they grabbed my bags and walked me inside the house. I wanted to continue staring at the outside first, but they wouldn't let me. Even pictures wouldn't ever do this place justice!

As we entered the mansion my eyes could forever remain open. My jaw unlocked almost as if I saw a ghost. "Do you like?" Martin asked. I was speechless—words couldn't describe my sensation. They could ask me the same question tomorrow and I'd still remain clueless as to what to say. I walked around almost as if I was dancing, and I smiled like a child in an amusement park—this is where I'm staying.

> ### *Aslan:* Of course

The scent in the house was of five-star meals and tea. The thought of tea reminds me of home—it certainly does. "Would you like water, juice or soda?" one of the ladies with captivating beauty asked me. "Cocktails please— just joking. Some soda would do! Thank you!" She then walked to one of her friends and mumbled something. I think they were gossiping about me—that's what I get for joking around. "Don't worry. They like you!" Martin said with a rather large smile on his face. "Allow Layla to show you to your room, and then I'm sure your father will return soon." Martin said. "Where is he?" "Dealing with some business—don't worry."

As Layla and I walked toward the stairs that lead to the bedrooms, I asked her who my father was and she said, "Very big man. Very important." Alright, I guess that was enough info, for now. Everything in this house was pristine—and I do mean everything. The only thing I haven't seen yet was a swimming-pool but it's alright. We arrived at a door on the left-hand side and before she opened it I shut my eyes—I love surprises. Anyways— back to what I was saying about the door:

When she opened it I quickly removed my hands and saw more perfection. The bed was huge and the window was big enough to allow the sun to hit me right in the face. I walked around and I couldn't complain and then I found a room that lead to the bathroom. My very own en-suite bathroom—what more could I want? Before I could do anything else I heard "Beverly ya habibti. Are you here?" What were the things he said after my name? My mother says that too. Is that my father? "Yella, go— your father is here!" Layla said to me while shoving me toward the door with her hands. But I was shy for a second because I was afraid—of whom I was going to meet now. I couldn't keep him waiting and so I walked toward the stairway.

In front of me stood a man twice my height. He was very handsome. He wore a suit almost as though he returned from a business meeting. We both stood there in utter silence while staring at each other. I felt something—but I don't know what. "Is—is that you?" he stuttered in complete shock. "Is it you, father?" We stood there for two fine minutes before we dashed into each other's arms. "I never thought I'd see you again—your mother just left without a word." He said while embracing me with tears flowing out. "I never knew—if I knew then what I know now, I would've sent you letters and visited you." I said. "No, that was *my job*. It's a mistake I made and I'm sorry—will you ever forgive me?" he asked.

Hold on just a minute I thought. Things are moving fast—and I still have other inspections to fulfill. "We shouldn't go ahead of ourselves just yet." I said while

I smiled at him. "Whatever you want—how was the flight?" "Splendid." "Any trouble with the chauffeur?" "Nope, everything was alright." He then quickly hugged me again and started to cry—and then I cried too... I couldn't help it. "Have you eaten yet?" he asked. "Not yet—but I'm famished." "What would you like? Just tell me and I'll have the Chef make it."

> **Yella:** Come on
>
> **Ya habibti:** Sweetheart

"I'd like some tea with croissants *please*." I said. "Over here we call tea: Shai. Your mother's favorite food was Croissant!" he said while laughing. And it still is. It's funny how a complete stranger gave me such a warm and fuzzy feeling inside, maybe it's because he could be my father? "Feel free. My home is your home. Anything you need please just ask." I'm beginning to love it here even more hence the permanent smile on my face.

"You're so grown now—Ma'shallah." he said. "My mother always says Ma'shallah, just not to me so much! She said it means 'thank you God.'" "Yes, something equivalent!" he replied. "I'd like to freshen up before I eat." "You have towels, soap and everything else in your cupboard." He said. "Thank you! I won't take a lot of time I promise" I said while I hugged him again. "You're Angelina's daughter... of course you'll take time." he joked, even though he was mucho correcto. Wherever my Spanish came from—I must have heard that in movie.

Did I mention the television in my room? The Plasma that's attached to my wall. I can't see myself falling asleep easily in there. I threw myself on the bed as I screamed right into the pillow. Is this really happening? I then walked toward the window to capture the beautiful view—I took pictures of my room and everything in it. I then slowly took of my clothes while dancing and then walked into the bathroom. I opened the big red cupboard only to find towels, three various choices of perfume along with tooth-brushes and many more… I am happy.

I slowly entered the shower and turned the water on. Feeling the warm drops against my back never felt better. I began to think of mother and my *friends* back home and then I tried to picture myself with them.

The feeling of being far from everything and everyone you know isn't as inevitable as you may think. Thinking of home leaves me questioning my being here, because if he *was* my father wouldn't I feel at home? But then again I've never had to leave my mother behind—ever. And then there was Amanda's absence; maybe that's why I'm so nervous…homesick.

Bathrooms tend to contain a simple look to them, but not this one. Mine has a marble floor and wall—almost transparent. The lighting will decrease your age by ten percent, and the space is more than enough to practice a scene from "Hamlet." The mirror is rather large and precise—I say "precise" because it precisely reflects my appearance.

I quickly wore my clothes as I remembered that lunch was ready. The odor roaming around the house was utterly magnificent—never have I inhaled anything like it. I followed the scent as it directed me toward the kitchen, and there sat my father upon my arrival. "Finally—I thought you slept in the bathroom." he joked. "I'd be a fool to do so because I'd miss out on this ever-so beautiful meal set for me—where do I start?" I said.

"This is Asida." he says as he points to a rather round-white thing that resembled hard mashed potato—loads of it overlapping each other. I stared at it with no further questions on my mind. "*That* is chicken Curry." I said as I excitedly pointed at the bowl filled with my delicious food—at least I'm aware of it. "Ha-ha...obviously!" he replied.

You also have an option of rice; bread; and or lasagna—later you can have chocolate cake for dessert, if you want" he said. "They all look very delicious—but are those *pancakes*?" I asked as my eyes opened wide. "Ha-ha! You can have those in the morning, if you like. This thing that you point at, with such curiosity, is called *Kissrah*. You can use it like bread, only it's very thin." he says as he points at. It really was something that appeared as a pancake...but it wasn't—sadly!

I slowly reached for the chicken-curry, and rice. I think trying the food I know best is the right direction to take. "The food won't eat you. We killed the chicken twice before cooking it!" he joked again. So he's a joker isn't it? I remember when Mother said we mustn't play games, or joke, around food—she found it very disrespectful. *"Be saha.* "He said. "What does that mean?" "It means, <u>blessing</u>." he replies. *"Be saha."* I said while scooping rice on my plate as though I was deprived of food when I was in London. He laughed and said, *"Ma'shallah*—you speak Arabic very well." "No, I don't. There's just a few things that I can say." "You will learn very soon, Beverley— your mother hasn't taught you much Arabic?" he asked. "No, she hasn't. She didn't really think Arabic would be relevant in my life." "Why is that? What is wrong with Arabic?" he said with a rather displeased facial gesture. "I never asked."

"Do you like to shop?" "Of course!" I replied, with an answer that only very daring girls would oppose to. "Martin will take you to the mall tomorrow—choose whatever you please." The smile on my face, stretched from ear to ear, proved my insanity for shopping sometimes...I'm a "shopaholic now," if you will.

"Thank you." I said as I reached for the glass of water. "But, of course—you don't have friends here. Martin shall take you to the British Embassy, and you will meet new people. I want you to be the happiest girl alive." he said as I blinked my eyes twice in disbelief. I had to pinch myself, but this really was real. I'm here and I'm—Oh right, I'm his daughter...or am I?

As famished as I was from the beginning of the day—I certainly had no further complaints right now. I am f-u-l-l. The maids cleared the table and then my father had to leave again. I didn't know where to, but mother always told me to never ask a grown person 'where they are going, and when they will return.' All I know is I'm super excited for tomorrow—what a day it shall be. How are the other kids in that British Embassy? Will they wear clothes like me, and will they have the same accent? They say that 'curiosity killed the cat,' but without curiosity life would be boring...just like the streets of London during rainy days.

The night approached us and it really was beautiful. The weather is exquisite and I wish I could swim right now. If I were back home a bunch of lads would go skinny-dipping—not something very sophisticated but it's fun anyway—looks fun I mean.

"Would you like anything?" Layla asked. "No, thank you. I'm alright—where's Martin?" "Martin is with the guard behind the house. Why?" "Oh no, I'm just asking." As Layla walked away I took a glimpse of the house again and then I shut my eyes. I swirled around and hummed to my favorite song by John Mayer.

My arms felt incredibly light—almost as though I could fly if I tried. When I opened my eyes I couldn't help but notice Martin's silhouette before me. "Do you need a dance partner?" he joked. "You like to stare at woman dancing?" "I don't see a problem with your dancing—so why not admire it?" he joked. I *was* impressed by his intelligence, I won't lie.

The next day was hectic, in my mind. I had to choose something extravagant to wear... I had to look good today! I chose my floral skirt, with prints of red and white roses, I love roses, they always remind me of my favorite park back in London. I then wore a white vest and my black stilettos with a thin belt around my waist-line. I felt rather ravishing! I walked my way to the kitchen and I found real pancakes ready for me. Syrup; honey; jam; butter; juice; toast and water were all set on the table....amazingly and very gratifyingly! I love the way the syrup oozed down my *oesophagus* (throat, for those of you who would desperately reach for the dictionary by now), and the smell of the pancakes were breath-taking. I could eat everything here if I weren't wearing such a tight and yet flattering outfit. If only Amanda was here now to enjoy this too.

"You look beautiful. *Inti helwa ya habibti.*" Layla said. "Thank you, but please translate the other sentence." "*Inti helwa yahabibti* means you are beautiful sweetheart." I was flattered to an extent of which I cannot elaborate...I was blushing even. "Are you ready to go?" Martin said as he walked into the kitchen, looking as good as usual. "Yes, let's go shall we?" I grabbed some pancakes and rolled them up.

"I like your outfit Beverly." Martin said. "Shukran." (which meant 'thank you') I replied while staring at my skirt. He was surprised that I knew a word in Arabic without it being translated for me. "So are you ready to meet new people today?" "Yes—I'm very excited!" "Just be careful, alright?" he said as he, dramatically, lifted an eyebrow. "What do you mean?" "You know very well. We need you to return home as safe as possible." "But anything can happen in six months, Martin—okay, I'll be careful." I quickly said. "Alright then."

The weather was quite warm today but it was comfortable. The car-windows were shut since the air-condition was on. Images of my friends in London conquered my mind for a minute—could I be missing them this much, that I must constantly think of them? I miss Amanda the most because we did everything together...we even— "We're here, Beverley." Martin interrupted my thoughts as we arrived at the mall first. "This is Afra." It's one of the biggest malls here. "Alright, let's go shop then." I said as he stepped out and opened the door for me.

The mall was rather large with a garden surrounding it. The inside was clean and there were escalators here and there, along with Christmas decorations. This was utterly captivating. The shops were everywhere and I couldn't wait to shop now. I need to buy some clothes for my next destination, even though that's in 6 months. All I know is the fact that the weather will differ—drastically.

The first thing I bought was a dress, and then everything else was very casual—but in a sophisticated way of course. I saw these amazing stilettos that I *had* to buy. It had very high heels and fuchsia snake skin, with a very cute strap; Amanda would love it. I approached the counter with her potential new shoes and I told the lady I wanted them. "Where is the Jewelry store?" I asked Martin. "Upstairs. What do you need?" I have an obsession with bracelets, and I need a new one right now. "Bracelets." he replied.

As Martin carried my bags, my head was spinning from all the lovely shops in sight. Of course I wanted to dash to the Jewelry store, but I wanted to enjoy everything on the first floor. We stepped on the escalators on our way up, and then I spotted the jewelry store. When we entered the store, my eyes were glued to the beautiful jewelry! I then walked around in search of bracelets, and then *there they were.*

I gasped as I caught sight of the most perfect bracelet. It had a diamond rose on it. The inside was engraved—with something that I've only seen in London—not the same of course. This bracelet had to be in my possession, I thought, as I stepped aback before I was blinded by its shine. "This bracelet just came in the store today morning." the lady behind the counter said. It's going to leave the store today too, I thought. "Really? It's really nice—I want it." I said. "It's ten thousand dollars." she says as she stares at me, up and down. I don't remember asking for the price. Those who ask for prices can't afford the object. "I will take it." I said as my eyes were glued to the bracelet. "Is it for *you* or for somebody else?" she asked. I tried the bracelet on and said, "for me," with a huge smile on my face. "I love it!" yelled Martin. "I love it too!"

"Alright, I think I'm done for now—can we please go to the British Embassy now?" I asked Martin. "Yes, of course."

Before we exited the mall, I bought two bottles of water... one for me and another for Martin. He had three bags on each hand and I carried our bottles of water. As soon as we stepped out of the mall the blaring sun-light hit my eyes and I quickly wore mother's stylish Dior sunglasses...I now feel ready! On our way to the British Embassy I noticed a person jogging, and then I said, "the last time I jogged was—never." Martin quickly stared at me, and then said, "honey, *you* don't need to even jog. *You're perfect*!" Today was all about being complimented!

"Are you hungry? Maybe we can stop somewhere so you eat first?" Martin asked. "Nope!" All I wanted to do now was to meet new people—I just had to! "What's it like in London?" My thoughts paused for a minute and then I stared at him and said, "different—very. It also rains a lot there. We have double-decked buses and loads of stores filled with haute couture—my mother's favorite." "Wow. Can I visit you someday?" he asked. "It would be splendid if you did." We both smiled. Moments later we arrived at a large gate. "Is that the British Embassy?" "Yes. Good guess!" Well, the flag was quite visible, and it would take a fool or a blind chap to not realize it. I noticed foreign people walking in and out of the Embassy and I felt more at home, all of a sudden. As Martin drove his way into the compound I anxiously waited for the car to come to a halt. I stepped out without him opening the door this time. I looked around as though I was expecting someone special to be there.

"Beverley. Remember what I said!" Martin yelled. "Yes, I know." "I'll return after one hour." he said as he handed me a gadget. "Here. If anything is wrong just press the red button and I'll be here soon." How fancy— so it's like I'm James Bond or something. "Thank you!" I said, as I tried to keep my cool. "Have fun." he said as he drove away.

Alright so I'm alone now—finally. I took a deep breath and then exhaled, before I walked my way to the strangers inside. The building was rather large and the inside was quite clean. I heard English accents here and there and I felt at ease. I spotted a tall man in his late twenties and I said, "hello. I'm Beverly Whatman." "Good Afternoon. You must be looking for the…teen-centre, correct?" He read my mind quite precisely. "Yes, I am." "Second floor—the elevator is to your right. You may ask the lady at the reception if you have more queries." He said. "Alright—thank you!" "Cheers." Did he say cheers? It's been a while since I've heard *that*.

As I walked toward the elevator I heard people yell, clap and probably kiss. "What's going on?" I asked the lady at the reception. "Soccer." she replied as her eyes were glued on her manicured nails. I completely forgot about soccer. The fanatics we are—we are slaves for soccer and fashion. I entered the elevator and pressed number two and then I waited while the typical elevator music was playing. Ding—the sound the elevator made as I reached my floor. Alright, here I go.

As soon as I stepped out, I heard hip/hop, people laughing and yelling…the type of noise we youngsters make. As I walked toward the noise I spotted vending machines and then I saw a very handsome chap. He was standing next to a vending machine, and I believe he just bought a candy bar of some sort. I was too shy to introduce myself to this tall, dark, handsome and athletically built creature. "Hello." he says as I walked past him. "Hi." I quickly replied.

I walked into the room where most of the teens were. There were some in the corner kissing while others were gossiping. There was a gang of boys and girls singing and rapping to music, and then I gasped when I saw an utterly beautiful, tall blonde—I had to introduce myself to her! I swallowed my pride and then I walked toward her. She reminded me of Samantha.

"Hey, my name is Beverley Whatman." She stared at me almost as though she knew me and then she said, "cheers. I'm Hariett Gambsey." Her plump cherry lips and her brown eyes were so seductive. "Hey I'm Lindsey Keeves." a bubbly, dirty-blonde blue eyed girl said as she approached us and reached out a hand that needed to be shook. "She's Beverly Whatman." Hariett said. "Lindsey and I are friends—where are you from?" "London." "Ditto." They both replied. "But I still live here" Lindsey said. "Yeah, and I'm only here for vacation." "Me too!" I replied with excitement.

"Have you met Christopher yet?" "No—should I?" I asked. "Oh yes—you'll meet him very soon." "So you live here? What do you do?" I asked Lindsey. "Well I study at the American School—eleventh grade" Lindsey replied. "There's loads of things and people to do." she continued. "People to do, huh?" Hariett asked. "No, you perv—you know what I meant!" Lindsey quickly replied in defense. "We go to clubs and stuff....and to the mall!" "I've been to Afra, today." "That's old news..." Hariett replied.

"How come you know so much, when you're only on vacation?" I asked. "Well my parents live here. I used to live here too, but I left two years ago after graduating High School." Hariett replied. "She studies fashion." Lindsey muttered as she walked toward the vending machine. "Oy—It's Fashion Design!" Hariett said. "So when are *you* returning to London?" she stared at me while awaiting a reply, a plausible lie. "In six months." I said as I stared into her hazelnut colored eyes. "Well, just be rest assured that those months will be the best ever." My eyes then lightened up as soon as those words immigrated into my ears.

"Have we met?" I then felt a spasm when I heard that deep familiar voice behind me. "Hey!" Hariett said, as she reached for a glass of fruit-cocktail. When I turned around, I realized that it was the vending machine chap. "No. We haven't actually." I said. "Christopher, Beverley, Beverley, Christopher." Hariett said as she sipped on her fruit-cocktail. We shook hands and then he winked at me as my heart sunk and the butterflies in my belly went wild.

"How old are you?" "nineteen—and a half." "You're from London, right?" "Yes, how'd you know?" "Well, I can tell from your accent." he said as he fluffed Hariett's hair. "You and your bag of lies—Lindsey told you, didn't she?" Hariett exclaimed." "How could she, when she's over there and I'm over here—smart ass!" he replied.

Judging from their outfits, they must be very wealthy too—or at least their parents are. I can smell their floral scented perfumes and his musky cologne too. For a second I forgot about Amanda and my other friends. Does that mean I'm not a true friend and that whenever

I find something good I'd leave whatever I already have, for the new thing? "Are you here to stay?" he asked. "No! Well actually, I'm leaving to Zanzibar in six months." Christopher had a shocked look on his face. "You can't be serious!" "Why?" I asked. "Because my best-friend lives there." Alright, so we do live in a small world after-all. "That's amazing really!" "*Oh jolly.*" Hariett said while she played with her straw.

"Oh I see, you've finally met him!" Lindsey said as she hung onto Christopher's back. "Why don't you come with us on Friday?" "Where to?" "Out—to the clubs and such." Hariett replied. "I'd love to, but I'll need to ask my father first—well he's almost not really my father." "So he's your stepdad?" Lindsey said as she reached for a glass of fruit-cocktail. "No, not quite." "I'm confused." Hariett said. "Well, I'll explain later." I said. "Do you want a fruit-cocktail too?" "Is there alcohol in there?" "No." "Alright then, hand me one!"

"Have you spoken to the others over here yet?" Christopher asked. "No—I'm not that interested now that I've met you guys." "Very picky, aren't you?" I licked my lips as I tasted what I thought was alcohol—it can't be! I tried to ignore my intuition and then I replied to his question. "No. Not quite. I'm just feeling a four musketeer's thing over here." I said.

"Ha-ha! That's *almost* so cute!" Hariett said as she swayed left to right. "Slow down on the *fruit* cocktail, snow-cake. You're about to fall over." Lindsey said. "There's no alcohol in there—" I said. "Or is there?" I guess that explains my sudden woozy sensation. "We should definitely hang out again." Christopher jumped. "Of course!"

"Do you have any siblings?" "Nope!" "A boyfriend?" Christopher asked, as he nudged Hariett. "No—not yet." "Oh? Someone's on a mission isn't it?" Hariett yelled while winking at me. I looked at the time on the square-shaped clock on the wall: It was time to go! As much as I wanted to stay, I had to abide by the rules—for now. "I'm leaving now. It was great meeting you guys!" "Already?" they said together. "My driver is here." "Well where are you staying?" "At my father's *mansion* in Amaraaaaaat!" I sarcastically said. "Oh really—we stay in Amaraat too—but *she* doesn't though!" Hariett replied while pointing at Lindsey. "Message us your digits and such." Lindsey said as she handed a note with phone numbers before I left. "Alright. Bye!" "Ta-ta." Hariette said, as she swayed her hand like a queen.

I found Martin awaiting my arrival. He was standing against the car almost as though I was his lover and he was expecting a kiss of some sort. "How was it?" "Funnyky." I paused and then wondered what the heck I just said. "Is that a *pure* English word?" He asked. I dramatically lifted an eyebrow and said, "I meant to say that it was fun." "Aha." he said as he grinned at me. I cleared my throat and entered the car as he opened the door for me. When we drove off I then remembered something—the cocktail I drank consisted of alcohol. I could've sworn that Christopher said there wasn't any alcohol! I think I just misinterpreted him...I was probably too focused on what Hariett had to say.

That was the first time I drank, ever since Frederick died. I can still taste the fruit in my mouth and then I slowly licked off the taste of alcohol. Is it true that bad habits die hard?

"Are you alright back there?" Martin asked as I stared out of the window as though I were lost. "Do you believe that bad habits die hard?" he kept quiet and then said, "well, it depends on the person—if you're a murderer it could take a long time to refrain yourself from continuing that habit—but at the same time, it could just be a permanent habit." "And what if you used to abuse yourself with alcohol and drugs?" I asked as he quickly turned around and confidently said, "then *that* calls for rehab." Even though I sat there asking questions as if I were completely oblivious to the answer, I knew that if someone else were to answer it for me I could have a chance of completely succeeding in this life.

"So—what were *they* like?" He said. I smiled and said, "nice." "Listen, I don't want to tell you, but I will—you're father has a surprise for you. A big surprise!" I quickly moved closer to the driver's seat and whispered, "what is it?" "Why are you whispering you silly thing?" I moved back and then removed a strand of hair from my face. "I can't tell you *what* it is though. I'm sure you'll find out today or sometime this week." We both shrieked as our excitement was felt throughout the car.

We finally arrived at home but then I noticed a red car. "You have a visitor here." I was a bit shocked. "Me? Already?" "Well the family wants to see you too, you know?" Phew... I was a bit confused for a minute but I'm glad someone wants to see me. Martin opened the door for me as I was hasty to enter the house. "Where are my bags from Afra?" "In the house, Beverley."

The door was opened by Layla as she mumbled to me, "*she is here.*" I didn't understand why she mumbled or who she was referring to. Even if I did know who it was, why was she speaking of *her* as though she was Cruella De Ville? "Who?" I asked. "Beverley *ya sucre!*" I heard a voice yell from the inside of the house. "Good luck." Martin whispered as Layla walked into the house with a broom. Alright, I'm afraid now. Frankly it seems as though I should jump off a cliff as opposed to meeting her. "Hello?" I said as I entered the house. In front of me stood a tall and subtle woman—a beautiful elderly woman standing there with her arms wide open. Are you kidding me? I thought! Is this what the hype was about out there? She seems like an angel....

I ran into her arms as though I knew her. Maybe it was the fact that I don't have a grandmother, or because I don't know of her. "Beverly—you're so big now!" *Now?* What did she mean by *now?* Maybe she saw a picture of me somewhere or something. "How is your mother?" she asked while she searched her purse for—something. "She is well—you know *her?*" She lifted her head and stared into my eyes as she said, "your mother was my angel...and now I don't know what happened to that angel." I stood there in shock. I was confused but I felt loved at the same time....somehow.

"Have you eaten anything?" "Yes." "Where is Philip?" she asked. Who is that? I thought as I tried to answer the question in my head, without seeming like a nut. "Philip?" "Your father." "Oh, of course—I don't know." She exhaled and said, "As usual. He's always out, out, out. Busy working hard for his money. No time for games." It made sense, judging by his luxurious lifestyle. Mercy, the other maid, walked into the room with a glass of wine which was then handed to my *grandmother*. "But what does he do?" I asked. She swiftly took the glass and said, "Career?" as she sipped on her red wine. "Government things." That was the only thing she muttered, and I didn't want to ask more questions about my father's career.

"How is school? The love life?" She seemed pretty cool for a grandmother—if she *is* my real grandmother. I stared at her perfectly parlor-combed hair, and her flawless skin. "I just graduated from High School—my love life? It's quite complicated actually—uhmmm." "Well, I'd love to continue this conversation but I must go. I have an appointment at the spa and I can't miss this one. Would you like to join me?" Of course I wanted to, but I didn't want to seem hasty. "No, thank you…Maybe next time." I said as I smiled at her. "*Wallahi?* But please do eat something before you faint. Drink a lot of water." She said and before she stepped out she whispered, "Don't fall for Martin, *ya habibti*." The door was then slammed shut before I could ask, "why not?"

Ya sucre: Sugar

Wallahi: I swear (honestly)

I walked into the kitchen and asked Isam, our chef, if he could re-heat the lasagna from last night for me. "We don't save food." That seemed like a waste, but then atleast my food would be fresh. "Would you like something else?" "Surprise me!" I said as I grabbed a bottle of water from the rather large, silver, refrigerator. "Is there wireless internet in the house?" He then stared at me as though I were insane and then he said, *"Tabaan"* with his thumb up.

I waltzed to the stairway, and then I quickly took a sprint upstairs right into my bedroom. I turned on the tele, and then removed my laptop from its bag (given to me by mother as a late graduation gift). The sounds of the birds chirping outside kept me at ease as I quickly imagined my park back in London. "Facebook" was the first website I had to visit. I quickly searched for the names: Hariett Gambsey, Lindsey Keeves and Christopher—I was utterly oblivious to his surname—maybe he told me but I forgot! Either way, I'll just search for him on Hariett or Lindsey's friends list, seeing that they were mutual.

Wow—five messages and all of which were from Amanda. "ARE YOU THERE? REPLY TO ME ASAP CUPCAKE." The other messages read, "I miss you. I MISS YOU. I MISS YOU. Have you forgotten about me ALREADY? I see that you've moved on with new friends." The girl has gone nuts without me.

I searched for my new friends, and I learned something new... Hariett and Christopher are...wow...related? That's insanity! Why was I not told? But then again we've only known each other for an hour. They didn't have to completely confide in me. I didn't so why should they? I sent them a friend request and then remembered that I needed a new number here. I then opened the window, widely, and yelled, "Martin!" being quite fortunate that he was there with the guard. He came running as though I was screaming for help. "What's the problem?" "Can you please bring me a new number for my phone?" "No need." he replied

What does he mean by, no need? "Why *not?*" I asked as I rested my hands on the windowsill. "Because you already have one. Check on top of your desk." "Thank you!" I yelled as I turned around. I must have been blind not to have seen the card on the table. I grabbed the card and read the charge-up instructions too. There was a knock on the door: "Beverley. Your food is set. Would you like to eat on the kitchen counter, or on the dining table?" Layla asked as she stood by my door. "Kitchen counter please. Simplicity is best." It took me five whole minutes to charge up my phone. I quickly jotted down my new number and forwarded it to Hariett and the rest of her crew.

I walked down the stairs and into the kitchen. The smell surrounding the house was mind-blowing. "This is chicken fillet stuffed with cheese and ham. To the side you have spaghetti and, my favorite, chicken curry." he said as I sat on the counter with an open jaw, again. I couldn't wait to taste this delicious looking meal! "Thirsty?" "Yes—Cola, please." I took my time as the cheese and ham oozed down my (ehhm) oesophagus.

> **Tabaan:** Of course

The spaghetti was professionally coated in chicken curry...*delicious!* I closed my eyes and remembered my mother's, sometimes, home-cooked meals. The way she would coat every meal in honey before it was cooked—very flavorful. "I love this." I said as I continued eating. "Thank you." "No, no—thank *you.*"

I then heard a sound that I haven't heard in days... it was the sound of a message I received on my BlackBerry. It felt good knowing that I can now network, again. It was a text from Hariett. Suddenly my heart began to beat fast, and I didn't understand why. She wrote, "please send me your address, love. We might pass by later on for tea or so. XOXO" Who is "we." Are they all coming or was she referring to her and her "brother" Christopher? "Isam, what is the address of this house?" "I don't believe the address can just be given off to strangers." "I'm not a stranger." "I'm not talking about you." He said while twirling a spoon. "They are my friends. They want to visit me." "This could cost me my job." "I won't tell on you—I promise."

He then gave me the address and I quickly forwarded it to Hariett while I anticipated her reply. "We're practically neighbors...see you in a jiffy! XOXO" she quickly replied. "Thanks for the meal, Isam." "No problem." I wonder how that would be said in Arabic. "Can you please translate that in Arabic for me?" *"Mafi mushkilla."* Wow. It sounds like a tribe of some sort!

Ding dong—the sound of the bell.

Two minutes later I heard "...Harriet...fi mushkilla?" Oh hold on, I ran to the door and said, "She is my friend. Please let her in." The look on the guards face was not pleasing. He looked as though somebody cursed his family or something. He turned around and walked toward the gate—as soon as he opened it, Hariett stepped in first followed by *Christopher.*

"Beverley! Nice place!" Christopher yelled as Hariett stumbled over a stone. "Are you alright?" "Oh yes... never mind!" she said. "Yeah, never mind the clumsy one." Christopher muttered. Of course we air-kissed, as though we were all mutual friends forever, and then we entered the house. "How come you didn't introduce him as your brother?" "Well you never asked." Hariett said as her eyes wandered. "Well that's the point of introducing someone." I said as I rolled my eyes. "Well, he's my step-brother! Happy?" she joked. "I love how we have such chemistry." "This is not a date lover boy." Hariett said as she patted Christopher's head.

"Are you guys thirsty or something?" "Water for me." "Cola for me please." "Layla, please bring us water and cola. We'll be in my bedroom...thank you!" Hariett then took a quick glimpse at the house again and seemed impressed. Our home is a bit smaller than this. Do you have a pool?" It seemed like a competition all of a sudden. "No." "Well *we do.*" she said as she stared at Christopher. "You guys came here fast, isn't it?" I asked. "Well, I think she told you we would be here in a *jiffy.* When Hariett says that, just know that she means it."

> **Mushkilla:** Trouble
>
> *Mafi Mushkilla:* No problem

We walked toward my bedroom and the first thing they said when they entered my room was "amazing view!" "I have a view of the pool." Hariett said. "I have a view of nothing but the garden." Christopher replied. I had to end this comparison game, and so I asked, "how long were you lads here, in Sudan." They both stared at each other and said. "Four years." "We visit every Christmas for the holiday, but this year we came a bit early because we'll celebrate Christmas in London." "Interesting—well I do believe my Christmas will be here." I confidently said. "We could probably visit you or something since you're here for long!

"By the way, Christopher, what do you study?" "The soccer ball and the field." I thought he was metaphorically speaking, but I guess not. "You're a soccer player?" "We've got a David Beckham at home." Hariett joked as she sat on my bed, grabbed my remote, and turned the tele on." Don't flatter me...I try my best!" he said as he walked into my bathroom.

High School graduates—one studies fashion while the other plays soccer... how ironic! "How come you have an American Accent?" I asked as I stared at Christopher. For some reason he stared at Hariett, almost as if to receive some approval. The funny thing was, she nodded, and then he turned back to me. "Well, I'm originally

American but I was adopted when I was ten. I just didn't want to have a British accent." "Why not?" "It's just too poshy." Hariett and I laughed as he stood there with his hands on his hips. "You *chill* with girls too much—be careful before you turn into one." She joked. He looked offended. "My hand just *happened* to rest on my hip. You got a problem?" he said before returning in the bathroom. "No, no..." surely we did find it hilarious though.

It almost felt as though I knew them for a while... It was as if they were with me in the past, but I just don't remember where or exactly when. Were we destined to meet, or was it a coincidence? "What else have you done here?" Hariett asked as she swung the remote in the air, almost as if to navigate a signal. "Well I've been to Afra, like I said, and to the Embassy. That's about it." "Well, you've only been here for two days now, right?" she asked. "Something like that." "Come with us tomorrow." Christopher asked while still lingering around in the bathroom. "I thought it was on Friday?" Hariette asked. "We don't only socialize on the weekends you know?" Christopher continued. "We'll be going for a drive around and we'll possibly stop by the malls and such." "Interesting—I'm in. What shall I wear?" Hariett stared at me as Christopher exited the bathroom and walked toward the window with his arms still rested on his hips. "You don't need *our* advice." he said as his fingers pointed at me.

"What do you think of Khartoum, by far?" "It's beautiful—very different. I feel different here. Good." "Were you expecting wild animals in the airport?" Hariett asked. I paused shamefully and said, "Yes—but that's *really not* my fault." I then quickly grabbed both of their hands and whispered, "Let me be completely honest with you—my mother sent me here to search for my father." "Amazing… one of those mission things?" Christopher whispered. "In a way. I find it rather interesting but also saddening." "Why saddening?" "Well suppose I become close and dear to my, potential father here, and then he's not *really* my father—and then what?" "Exactly… and then what?" Hariett said as she giggled. "And then you continue the search, or you just stop and focus on your life. You're not a baby you know."

Christopher replied.

There was a knock on the door, and Layla entered with our drinks. "Are you hungry?" she asked as she placed the drinks on the table. "No, thank you." We all replied at once. As soon as she left the room, we continued our conversation. "But that's my reason for visiting Zanzibar and the other places after this." "Wow! Can I come with you?" Christopher joked as he jumped on my bed. "If you want to." I sarcastically replied. "Yeah, as if your bed would give you such a break." Hariette said to Christopher.

"I could use some cocktails right about now." Hariett said. "Speaking of cocktails" I said as I stared into Hariett's eyes, "you told me there were none in the ones we drank, at the Embassy." "Well I lied." She mumbled as she giggled. What a silly girl… *if she only knew!*

"Wait, so what time tomorrow?" Christopher asked. "Around two-ish in the afternoon. That's when Chris tends to awake—I'll call you though." "Can you teach me Arabic? I don't speak much of it" I asked "Obviously not." Hariett replied.

"By the way, you *do* know that they speak Arabic everywhere here?" "In a way." Christopher quickly turned his head toward me and vigorously but sarcastically asked, "in a way? Did you think they spoke Japanese or something?" "Well I wasn't exactly certain—nothing wrong with that."

"By the way, is Lindsey coming along tomorrow?" "She didn't tag along to your house… why would she join in a drive?" Christopher replied. "I just thought maybe—" "Nope. Hariett said. "She has plenty of home-work and stuff." She continued. It's almost as though Hariett was our spokesperson—as if she were the dictator. For some reason it felt as though we had to abide to her every say. "Anyway, Bev—*we gotta go.*" Hariett said as she jumped off my seat, as though she were a dwarf. "So soon?" Christopher stood up and said, "only because we have very important things to do..." and then he hugged me. "Tomorrow?" "Tomorrow it is!" I said. I then walked them all the way to the gate and then took a walk around the house alone afterward. I never noticed the space around this house.

I wish I owned a place like this. The closest I ever came to something like *this* was when I attended Meleny's birthday party. Meleny was *rich*—filthy rich. One of those superficial girls who really make you re-think your own lifestyle. My mother always told me to appreciate whatever I have, and to be grateful. I never quite understood that since she always strived for a richer boyfriend, each time. Mother was only happy when she received jewelry on her doorstep, or when she was surprised with a credit card. What really made her smile, ear to ear, was the fact that Harrods became a part of her daily routine.

Any man who was not in possession of a credit card, or a BMW, was not relevant to her. Somehow I believed that she wanted me to be like her! I've always blamed her for what happened to me... but then again how could I?

And then there was a sound of a horn by the gate, and I noticed it was my father's car. I'm glad he's back because we hardly spent time together, since my arrival. I waited for him by the door of the house and watched Martin open the door for him after the car was parked. I still have no clue as to what he does—but I was told that he worked for the government.

"I chose to remain in this maze for the value of the superficial…but we all know that superficial won't last forever."

"Beverly!" he exclaimed as he walked toward me with his arms open wide. I ran to him, almost like a child running into her father's arms. I was in need of Love. "Have you ever dreamt of Egypt?" he asked. "Never." "Do you have Egyptian friends—or do you know anything, at all, of Egypt?" "No." I replied as I stood there with my hands on my head, almost as if to shield the sun from my face. "We'll be leaving on Tuesday afternoon." I gasped as I held my hand over my mouth. "Serious?" *"Wallahi."* he replied. I jumped with glee and then I quickly ran all the way to the gate and back to him. "Why did you run?" he asked. I stood there out of breath. "To burn off the energy" I said as he laughed.

"I'm glad you love my surprise this much." "Yes I do—can I bring a friend or two along?" "Friends—all the way from London?" I smiled and said, "no... I met people at the Embassy." "Whatever you want, *ya hayati.*" *"Shukran."* I said as I hugged him again.

"Have you eaten anything?" he asked. "Definitely. I had a delicious meal! It was chicken curry and chicken fillet stuffed with ham—" he quickly then said, "and cheese."

The thought of "who father really is" crossed my mind every second as I stared at him and realized we had much in common. I refused to ask and I will not ask. Imagine the frustration or dilemma this may cause. Look at him, I thought to myself. Doesn't he look like you? I struggled to believe that this could be a misinterpretation of my mother's perspective. I was trapped in a maze of which I failed to escape. I chose to remain in this maze for the value of the superficial…but we all know that superficial won't last forever. In my being here; I've never questioned why he was always away…he doesn't quite seem as eager to see me, as I am to see him. Most people find this odd, but maybe this is how he reveals compassion? I've never seen it shown like this, but could it also be that he's scared? After a peculiar debate with my conscience, I then escaped to my room only to reside on my bed.

"Have you ever dreamt of Egypt?" I quickly texted Hariett. The sudden reply proved her excitement. "You're not saying what I think…" she replied. "Would you go there with me if I asked you to?" "Definitely…when?" "Tuesday-Friday." "You must be kidding—So soon?" I giggled to myself as I thought about the insanity in this. "My father surprised me with the idea. Just come—you and Chris." "OMG!" "You're welcome." "I…Love…You!" It's amazing how people abuse the word "love" when they receive something quite ravishing. I got texts, the whole night, from Hariett and Christopher about what they should to wear, and what they should take. It's as though they've never traveled before…even though I sound like a complete hypocrite now.

I could get used to this. Maybe I don't have to return to the life that I lived—the ever so excruciating life that only offered me little pleasure. The thought of mother being alone scares me, but she sent me here. I'm certain that this is what she wants. I'm far-away from pain and confusion, maybe this is what I need. They say that, "running away from problems never solves anything," but what if it could save my life? I've never asked for anything greater than love… so maybe this life is for me.

My eyes closed as I reminisced of what was and what could be… typical me! What is Egypt like?

The next morning was another beautiful day. Khartoum called my name and I was ready to respond. Today is the day that I'll be introduced to the African *glamour* and the endless fiesta. I reached for my phone and saw "1 new message." In excitement I read the message and it read, "not too sure about Egypt. We're meant to be in London for Christmas—remember?" Great, she just jabbed me in the heart with her stilettos. I replied, "we'll discuss when I see you," before I threw my phone on the bed and rushed in the shower.

There was no time for a long shower. I was excited and ready to enter the city. There's nothing better than having a credit card. It's not my money so there's no reason to worry about it—right? Before I could clothe myself, Hariett's rather obscene laughter, outside, gave me a spasm. They've arrived already. "Beverley! Bev! Come on!" They yelled as though they were in a park. In response to their ruckus I yelled back, "on my way down."

I had no time for brunch either. The fact that I wore jeans and a top was enough proof that I was in a hurry. It didn't matter—and it shant, because I look fine. "What happened to you? Did you forget about today?" Hariett asked. "No—I was in the shower and such." "Layla, I'll be out with my friends." "It's not like she's blind." Christopher sarcastically said. I stared at him with the most peculiar look. Their car was parked by the gate and it was amazingly expensive-looking. It was large and silver-ish. "I see the guard let you in this time. Who's driving? I see no chauffeur." I said as I searched around. "Me." Christopher replied with a smile on his perfect face. "I'm not ready to die just yet." "And I'm not ready to waste time just yet—let's go already." Hariett said as she grabbed my left hand.

"What the—" "Hariette." Christopher gasped as Hariett grabbed my hand. "Beverley?" "What?" "What's this?" she says as she vigorously grasped my wrist with a shocking look on her face. "Relax it's nothing." "Fucking hell—child." Christopher leaned forward. "What?" He asked. "Look at her fucking wrist." "Oh God…don't tell me you're one of those!" he said as I pulled my hand away and said "one of what? No I'm not one of anything." They both remained still, almost as though they were awaiting a reward. "Can we go already?" I said. "No. We shant." "What's the big deal? We all have secrets isn't it?" I paused in thought of what I just muttered. What shall I say now? Our friendship has only begun and it would be a shame if it were to end right now. I must tell them everything— but I can't. It feels as though my mind has been held

121

prisoner, and I must rescue it. Have I gone insane? "Let me breathe—I'll confide in the both of you when I'm at ease." I said. "As if we're the cause of this." Hariett said as she shoved her phone deeper in her pocket.

We finally entered the car after a mild but sour debate. "Are you alright?" Hariette asked as she stared at her reflection in the rear-view mirror. "Yes." I replied trying to conceal my potential breakdown. "I—never." And then it happened; I just brokedown there and then. The feeling I felt was too strong and I needed to confide in someone other than Amanda. She wasn't there right then, so I didn't know what to do. I just brokedown… "You never what?" "I never wanted all this to happen. I tried my best to stand my ground." I continued. "Slow down, what are you talking about?" Christopher asked as the car began to accelerate. "Slow down!" Harriet yelled. "We need to get to our place quicker so we can have a proper discussion." "Nothing—I don't know what I'm talking about." I said. Hariette then exhaled almost as though she grew tired of me already. "Give her time." He said.

I felt a sudden relief when the car stopped. "This is our place." "I thought we were going out?" "Not until you explain that!" Hariette said as she pointed at my wrist. "There's nothing to explain…just don't push it." "Let's go." I could feel their compassion, and I felt loved over and again—but I tried to shield myself from it. "Are you hungry?" "Yes." I said. We stepped out on a large property. I can't describe their home but smaller than Phillip's…I was broke down and I felt useless. "Carry yourself will you?" Harriet mumbled to me. The truth is that I didn't want to eat. I just wanted to explain what happened, and what's happening. Someone else had to know—I had to hunt for another perspective. Then one of the doors was slammed shut, and all I could hear was an echo. It almost felt as though I was in another atmosphere—I felt lost for a moment. "Do you need a doctor?" Hariette asked. I swiftly heard her words but her mouth moved slowly. "Hurry, Chris! Bring some water!" was all I heard after I found myself on the ground... It's happening again I thought. "How many fingers do you see?" Hariett asked while waving her fingers in my face. "I'm not crazy—I promise." "How many?" I took a breath and answered, "one." And then I noticed it was her middle-finger. "Good. Well fuck you for scaring me like this." She said. Oh the irony, I thought to myself.

Chris rushed to us as though to save a life—oh yeah mine of course. "She's up!" "Let's take her in the kitchen. Give her some water." The inside of the house was clean and occupied with things and more things. "To my room." Hariette directed. We slowly climbed heaps of stairs and finally arrived in her room...just as I expected: It was organized and perfume everywhere and a hint of cigarette smoke. "I'm alright, you can put me down now." "What happened out there?" Chris asked. "I don't know—maybe I'm just hungry?" "uhuh." Hariett said. "Mary, please make us fried rice and cake also." Hariett said on an intercom. "Do you have loyal friends in London?" I was oblivious to the answer only because I've never been asked this. Shall I lie? An answer was expected and here I am—debating with myself. "What do you mean?" "Do you have trust-worthy friends?" she continued. I felt harassed by a question I couldn't answer. "Yes." I quickly replied as I sat on her sofa. Hariette then sat next to me and asked, "who?"

I knew the answer was Amanda, but I couldn't say it. Maybe I don't have a trustworthy friend in London or anywhere. Hariette could be trying to teach me a lesson—but why, and what sort of lesson? The only thing I did was accept that *ticket*. I never traveled before but I saw it as an opportunity. I'm here now, and I'm being questioned for an answer I'm scared to answer.

*"I'd regret dying without trying to solve this puzzle
for dying itself is a puzzle we sympathize with."*

"Bev, who is it?" I gazed into her eyes and then I had flashbacks. "I'll tell you both, but I'll say this in confidence." They both nodded. "No-one else must know, and don't speak while I speak…I need to remember everything." I continued. "You're scaring me now." Chris nervously said. "Don't feel obliged to say anything, Bev." To have friends who will sit and listen to a life that I defaced on my own is a blessing—I thought. "No, I don't." I said.

Before I spoke again, I constantly stared back and forth, at them. I was scared and nervous… I didn't know what their reaction would be. My palms were sweaty and I began to shake. I then took a deep breath and exhaled…here I go. "My life used to be easy. I never had complications, or at least I didn't think so. I was good, and I played by the rules. I never had to worry about disloyal friends or family, nothing seemed easier. Before I was introduced to illegal fun, I was the type who sat in front of the class. I had a few friends, actually none at all, although I was intelligent. I never lied about kissing; sex; boyfriends; stealing, but only because I never encountered those things. I was blind. Literally blind"

They both gasped and stared at me. I then stood up and walked around the room and continued. "I was innocent. My brother in the other hand was not." "You were blind? You have a brother?" Hariett asked with a tear in one eye. I forced my hand out as a sign for silence. "He definitely wasn't. He liked the spotlight—and *chilling* with boys who liked bad things. He played with fire, and then got burnt. Life really isn't as complicated as we make it. You see, all we had to do was play by the rules, right? Obviously if you stepped out of line, there were consequences. My brother never kept consequences in consideration."

I grabbed a pen from Hariett's table and waved it around. "And then there was Amanda. Such a good friend she is. We've been through it all. There was a day when I was curious about sex, and then Amanda showed me what to do and how. That was the first time we ever did bad. But I liked bad, and I became addicted. Attending weekly parties and clubs was our new habit. Kissing boys and flirting were habitual…and then came sex—more! Even though Amanda showed me how, it definitely didn't feel the same as when *fucking* a guy." Hariett shook her head. "That wasn't half of it. I promised to never do drugs—I didn't want to be like my brother, Frederick." Chris began to chew on his gum faster, as though he was anticipating something bigger. "But of course when you learn from the bad, you become the bad. I drank cocktails to loosen me up at parties. You know how shy we get at times?" they nodded.

"Cocktails loved me, and I grew to love them." I stopped and thought to add something new, something made up, to see their reaction, as if the rest wasn't enough. "But things got out of hand, one night. I tried Ecstasy for the first time. I thought it would be the last, but I was wrong." I stopped waving the pen around and said, "and then I found myself in a hospital bed one morning. I looked around and there she was beside me. Amanda was there like a mother would be. Of course my mother came later on, but Amanda was first. She explained what happened, and I felt stupid. From that day onward I promised to leave the bad things…but of course bad habits die hard."

There was a sudden knock on the door and we all shrieked. "Come in!" Hariett screamed. It was Mary with the food. "Thank you." I grabbed my plate and continued my story, as Hariett and Christopher ate too. "These slits on my wrist" I said as I pointed with a knife; "this is what happens when there's no motivation—when you're left feeling inferior to everyone and everything." I paused and began to eat. The food tasted so good that I forgot where I was. "From cocktails to drugs—I didn't do hard liquor, and yet I landed on drugs. I became a junkie… believe it or not but *I was* hospitalized. This was not what I wanted, but it happened. The only thing that I had to do was learn from it. There was heartbreak, deception and one-night stands."

"The slits on the wrist?" Hariette carefully asked. "These I'll never forget. I was in juvenile prison for two weeks—both Amanda and I." This was a bit exaggerated— very, but I felt that I needed to. Hariette and Chris paused as their jaws dropped. "We stole some things, and we were also caught with drugs. We were lucky to have spent time in juvenile as opposed to the real thing. That's where I began to slit my wrist… right after I was beaten by a gang of girls in there. I told myself to be strong, to have faith, and here I am now."

"What about your brother?" I shamefully stared at the ground, as I swallowed the question with remorse. "I prayed every day that he would die, and then I got what I wanted, without wanting it anymore." "Why would you do that? He was your blood." Christopher said. "I know—I just didn't think it would happen. I only prayed for it because I was tired." I continued. "It's not for you to decide." He said. I began to cry; I thought they understood. "Everything happens for a reason, Bev. At least he's in a better place. I'm sorry for your loss." Hariette said as she embraced me. "I'm sorry too—but we're here for you." I needed an atmosphere like this. Being away from home changed me. I didn't want to return to the person I was. I thought that being here kept me from who I hated to be, even if it meant adding some lies.

"No offense, but my appetite is fucked up now. I wish I knew you before, so I could've been there for you. Amanda was not—" Harriet said as she then jumped when I banged the plate on the table saying, *"Don't talk about her. You know nothing of her."* "I just wanted to say that maybe she wasn't the right friend, at the time." Hariette said. I cooled down and returned to the bed. "She was the only friend I had…the only friend I thought I'd ever have."

"I'm so sorry it had to be that way. Sometimes life's so hard because we must learn from it. If it was so easy—nobody would be serious." Hariette explained.

"My mother tried to explain. She tried to be there, but it wasn't enough. I needed more than explanations. I needed her to be a mother—motivation. Anyone can explain anything." I said. "Did you talk to her about this?" "Not really—but it's too late now." "It's never too late until she dies." Christopher said. "Well thanks for putting it that way." I said as I wiped my tears.

"Crying won't solve this. What you need is motivation—like you said. We're here for you." "Thanks guys." "You know what?" Hariett said. "Tell." "About Egypt—I think I'll go. I'd rather be there with you then in bloody London where it rains twenty-four-seven." "Liar!" I screamed joyfully. "No really—Chris what'cha think? Christmas in Egypt sounds heavenly doesn't it?"

"I'm up for it. Explain that to mother and father." Christopher said. "That won't be a big deal." "Are you happy now that you know?" I asked. "No and yes." "Well I'm glad that that weight is off my shoulders." I said. "It's like a movie, if you ask me." Christopher said as he chomped on his cake. "Boys truly do think differently—do you still want to go out?" Hariett asked. "Of course. This story-telling really won't change my mood. It can't…it's nothing new." I said. "okay…" They both replied.

"Coming to think of it; I have friends who suffer the way you had." Christopher said. "How so?" "Well, they're delinquents and they do drugs along with the rest." "Same here." Hariette interrupted. "But your story is interesting in a very touching way. I never heard something like *this*. And you were blind? It's amazing that you aren't now. Wow." Christopher continued. "There's more to it anyway." I said. "After all that you just said?" Christopher asked. "I forgot to mention abuse." "You've been through it ALL isn't it?" Hariett muttered as she crossed her legs. "Who was the abuser? We'll get that fucker." "No one. Let's just let it rest."

"Sometimes it's better not to be a hero." Christopher said. "I'm not trying to." "What he means is, sometimes it's better not to always shield yourself. We all get hurt and learn from it. Learn to acknowledge pain—accept it. You'll learn from it." Hariett said. I hated the fact that she was right. I only increased the pain by pretending to be strong. Maybe I should've spoken of this before, but it wasn't my fault. Amanda already knew everything. You can't repeat the same thing to a friend—unless she isn't a true friend. Maybe that was it.

"I tried to commit suicide—plenty of times." They both remained silent. "The last time I tried was different, compared to the rest. This time I nearly did it. I remember gasping for air while trying to scream for help. People were around but they thought I was joking. Death isn't a game when it stares you in the face. That's when Amanda rescued me. That was my first time nearly dead. That's almost when I learned my lesson." The sound of their beating hearts was all I needed to clarify my insanity.

I wish I knew then what I know now. Maybe my life would've been easier that way. Maybe I wouldn't have been through that pain. Maybe, just maybe, would I have been smarter than I was. The thought of my vulnerability really hadn't fazed me until now. I stared at Hariette and Chris as I wondered whether I should conclude the story. I've already begun—it wouldn't really differ...I think. "Are you ok?" Christopher asked. I held on to my heart as I attempted to carry on with my history. "I...I" I couldn't' do it. I meant to, but the words wouldn't discharge from my mouth. I was afraid.

"You what...?" "I don't know what's wrong with me." I said. "All you need is a cup of tea." "Honestly, I need a psychologist and a priest." I continued. I failed to understand why a broken heart was all it took to deface a mind. Everything I've been through felt like yesterday's dream smothered in a haze of tomorrow. I've never been too certain of anything since I've learned that tomorrow is never promised. "Try to breathe in, and out. Everything will be alright!" Hariett said. I never thought the day would really come for me to be standing in a room confiding in someone or some people. There I stood, and never have I felt like that. I won't lie, it did feel amazing, but not quite. There's still one more thing that I want to express, but I can't.

Call me a coward if you want, but if you knew what was bothering me; you'd literally think differently. I want to be alone right now. My mind is ambushed by my own questions. If anyone understood me, they would understand why I'm like this. "If there's anything else you want to say, we're listening." Hariett said. I know they're listening, but maybe I don't want to say more. I was so confused that everything seemed senseless then. My actions weren't justified, or at least I didn't think so. I deserve a second chance and maybe that's what I'm getting. What happened before was not my fault. But somehow I kept blaming myself for it. I'm so confused, but at least you have an idea of why I'm this way.

I'm Beverley Whatman and I'm more complicated than most people. I'm indecisive and I'm a puzzle that can't be solved. "You're a puzzle." Harriett joked as she strayed a strand of hair from her face. "Yes, I am." I replied as Hariett bit her lips and tipped her head back a little. I couldn't help but stare at her lips, and wander. "Girls." Christopher mumbled as he opened a book.

"Anyway! About Egypt—what's the plan?" Hariett asked. "So you really want to come?" "Obviously." Christopher's attention was quickly captured again. "Egypt. This will be amazing—how long did you say?" "From Tuesday to Friday, I believe." "Christmas in Egypt—wonderful." "Take loads of bikini's and shorts—along with dresses, skirts and—" "and your brain." Christopher joked. "What time do we depart?" "The details are at home... but it should be in the morning." "I'm so nervous and excited at the same time!" Hariette screamed as she bounced on her bed. I felt the energy flow within the room and I can't say that I've felt that way...before then.

"Alright, we'll wait for the information." Christopher said. "Are you wearing *that* when we go out?" Hariett asked as she pointed at my clothes. "Well I didn't bring anything else along." I said as I tussled my hair. "I'll just lend you a piece." "Yeah, a piece of advice." Christopher mumbled. "No you dimwit. A sexy number I know she'll love." "Just say you have clothes for her—what's with the pieces and numbers?" Christopher joked. I turned to Hariett as I awaited a reply. "Stupid boy." Ha! Was that her comeback? Rather vague.

"This?" Hariette said as she stood opposite me with a red skirt and black top. "Red Light District-ish." I said. "It's not that bad." She replied. "Yeah, anything that shows skin isn't that bad for boys." Christopher muttered. "And this?" Harriet threw something at me. As soon as my eyes fell on that outfit, I knew that I had to have it. It was a sinfully short black dress, covered in diamante studs. "Wow." "That's what I thought when I first laid eyes on it." "Try it on." "What shoe size are you?" "thirty-nine." "Me too!" Hariette screamed as she fought her way through a pile of shoes.

"What will you wear?" I asked. "Don't worry about me, I've got this." Hariette replied. "I'll just wear this." Chris said as he began to randomly stretch his arms. I dashed into the bathroom and changed the dress. I felt amazing but I had a *bad* feeling about this. I ignored my intuition as I walked outside and showed-off the dress. "Ok, wow. That seriously perfectly fits and suits you." "In—deed." Christopher said. "Thanks. Thanks for making me feel amazing again." "And it's free too." Christopher teased.

"Try these on." I heard her say as shoes flew toward me before I caught them. "Sexy." "Glamorous…tonight is the night—forget your entire case of problems, babe!" It's easy for her to say. She's not the one trapped in a secret in which she could slowly drown in.

I could smile, but it won't change the fact that I'm living a lie. There were times when I felt as though my head were to explode—all because of one secret. There's more to it than just that, but words can never express my breakthrough.

"All the things I said really were nothing." I said. "Huh?" They stood there in confusion. "There's way more to it." I continued. "I can imagine." "Tell us what's burning your tongue?" Christopher asked. The words just won't come out. It could be the fear of them thinking less of me. This is the fear that I've faced throughout my life. "Don't feel pressured. Tell us when you're ready, babe." That's what I needed to hear…at least for now. "I'll get dressed in a bit, and then we'll be off." Hariett said. "Fuck, is it already five?" Christopher asked. "Time is escaping." I yelled in excitement. "Don't be such a loser, we're nearly done." "I bet if I take a nap and awake, you'd still not be done." Christopher said as Hariett pulled out her tongue at him.

Twenty minutes later and we were done. "Shall we go?" Christopher said as he obviously lost patience. "Let's go." Hariette looked rather captivating in her black and white dress plus her *Jimmy Choo* heels—she had a thing for fashion, that one. We quickly exited the house and drove away. "Where to?" I asked. "The place." Hariett replied. I couldn't help but have a bad feeling. I refused to question our destination but only because I *trusted* them. After the story I had told them, I knew that they would look out for me—just like they promised. I thought.

"Have you tried Shisha before?" It must have been one of those rhetorical questions. I sat there in silence as I tried dodging the question. Hariett then swiftly turned her head and repeated the question. "I could have." I quickly replied. "Well, it's either you have or haven't." If I said I have would I do it again? "...Haven't." I said. "Jolly." Hariette replied sarcastically.

Flashes of Amanda suddenly appeared before me, as though it was a sign of some sort. I've neglected her—I've forgotten the definition of friendship. "Do you suffer from that ADD thing or amnesia?" Hariett asked. That question lacked sense of compassion and intelligence. "So where exactly are we going?" I asked while making a timid facial gesture. "You wanna have fun right?" I nodded, as though they could see me. I felt trapped for a reason I couldn't seem to justify. My heart raced as though I was chased by a predator. It's senseless to say that they may have had a sour plan for me—so I just sat there and monitored their every-move, *before it all* happened again.

I swallowed my spit as though I were cornered by bullies, and clenched my fist like Mohammed Ali. For a second I wanted to stand my ground, but why? It's insanity I tell you. My nerves have been picked at and all I could do was sit and observe, like a child obeying her mother. I grasped the finished hem of the dress, and nervously occupied myself with it. "Would they even let her in?" "Probably—definitely." "In where?" I asked. "Shhh." Hariett silenced me for a while.

They were like strangers…unexpectedly. My eyes widened as Hariette hushed me. I was speechless right then and there. I closed my eyes to visualize the streets of London; the shops and the constant sound of heels beating against the ground…Amanda. I forget to mention mother, too. She's always been there for me, and she still is really. I've never seen another mother with the strength of a Goddess …she is my Goddess. There were times when we didn't get along, and other times when we were best friends. The only obstacle that stood between us is the secret that will forever haunt me… forever feed on my integrity. I'm lost.

Sometimes I— "Bev, are you hungry?" Hariette asked as my thoughts faded away. "Not quite." I longed for pizza and Banana milkshake. I stared around as we reached a rather dark alley. "Here! Put on some of this and that." Hariett said as she surrendered her lipstick and eyeliner. "I already—" "listen, you want to enter don't you? You gotta look a tad bit older." Hariett continued. Bollocks. Here we go again! I knew that applying this lipstick and eyeliner meant trouble. Why am I here? Wasn't I just in Hariett's room crying in confidence moments ago?

I exhaled and stared at Hariett. I couldn't see a spot of mercy in those eyes. "Come on!" she said. I won't do it…I can't! I'm aware of the consequences of that lipstick and shit-liner! I was aggravated but refused to show it. I continued staring as though I were lost. "Give it." I finally said. "It took you forever."

"Let's go. Remember that you're twenty and you left your ID at home." "That's it?" "We'll take care of the rest."

"I told you, didn't I?" Hariett said. "Yes." I replied as I stared around the room that was hosted by loud music and *alcohol*. "Danny!" Chris yelled at a boy. Before I could ask who he was, he sprinted toward him almost as though the Olympics took place. "That's Chris's friend." Hariett whispered. Yes, I can see that. But why are they so affectionate toward each other...how peculiar—boys are. "You dance much?" she asked. "Yes, but I'm thirsty actually." We headed toward the bar and before I could greet the bartender, Hariette yelled out, "tneen tequila." Tequila was all I understood. "No, no. We can't." I said. "Just relax—you've had a hard day, okay?" "Yeah, all the more reason to not drink?" I replied. "I can't and won't drink these two alone." She said. I stared at the weapons of mind destruction as I searched for an adequate reason to drink. Well I did have a hard day and one really can't do any harm. I then reached out for my glass with uncertainty: "Shukran ya habibti!" "Uhuh." I said.

Before my eyes blinked, I found myself on the dance-floor. Swaying my hips and bopping my head was all I could do. Hariett on the other hand was the perfect impersonator of a stripper, minus the pole. I thought it would be just *one* drink? The night was young and even though we loitered; that wasn't it. "Go with me to the loo—something I must show you." Hariette said as I quickly grabbed her hand as though my life depended on it. When we entered the bathroom, Hariett pinned me against the wall. With a demonic facial gesture she said, "I saw you checking me out-eh." I shook my head in disbelief. "So?" She slowly licked her lips and my palms began to sweat. "Kissed a girl before?" she asked. I slowly but indecisively nodded. She moved a bit closer and then her lips touched mine.

The feeling was, once again, exhilarating but I had to end this. "Stop!" She then moved aback and raised her eyebrow as she bit her lower lip. "Really?" She then furiously began to lick and suck on my neck—there was no turning back now. I began to moan…I liked it? Lucky enough nobody else was in there. I pulled her closer and she moaned louder than me. "Shhh, we're not alone." She said. "Shhh." She repeated. We both giggled at the insanity even though we enjoyed it. Before I knew it, her fingers lingered under my dress. Is this why she chose a dress for tonight? Goodness—she chose my whole outfit too.

I felt her finger penetrate me and I loved it with uncertainty. She moaned a bit louder as I returned the favor by lifting up her dress and cuffing her mouth. We began to play dirty little games—filthy I must say. "This feels better than when a guy does it." She whispered in my ear. Before I could reply I found her beneath me. She started to lick me slowly, and suck on me. I tried to pull her up just in-case anybody entered the bathroom…but I couldn't do it. I tipped my head back and closed my eyes.

Tneen: Two

Tneen tequila: Two Tequilas

The thought of somebody coming in really intensified the moment but I had to push her away.

"Nobody needs to know."
"Nobody?"
"Not a soul."
"Until death, you mean?"
"Maybe then."

Another secret really wasn't what I needed, but I cared to spare the humiliation. We dashed out of the bathroom with grins on our faces. Our giggling and laughing fooled the crowd… for now. "Where were you?" Christopher asked as he pointed his finger at us. "Doing girly stuff." Hariett replied as she nudged my shoulder. One would think that Hariett's alcohol intake was enough, but they would be wrong. She walked—I mean wobbled, to the bartender and demanded another drink. I couldn't understand how Christopher allowed that, but then again they're both *fucked* up in the head. Including myself.

For a second I ignored the incident in the bathroom… Not because I wanted to but because I've been through it before—it wasn't anything unfamiliar. "Bev! Another?" I heard an echo. Why did I hear an echo? Hariett then waltzed toward me and grabbed my hand. I can't exactly remember what she whispered in my ear, but I think it was, "I'd kill you if you told." To threaten a life for the value of your own really shook me, but that is just hypocritical. "What?" I asked. "It'll spill on you and it's cold" she said. I must've been insane to literally paraphrase that.

"I want to go home." I muttered as I tried to stand still. "Not yet—the fun has just begun." Ironically enough I already knew the answer, before I opened my big mouth. Before I could let out a big sigh my favorite song played. "Say" by John Mayer and it was all I needed to hear for now. "Care to dance." Chris asked. I stared at him and suddenly reminisced of Brian. "Yes." I shyly replied. He took my hand and then we began.

Brian was, kind of, my first love—I'd like to think so. He introduced me to sex and *alcohol*. It may seem insane to you, but I love him the way the sky loves the stars. Even if I were to see him again, I'm certain I'd fall in his arms. He knows of my secret, and so does Amanda. Brian was also the first to really break my heart... It's a feeling that can never be secluded from love—unless you're strong enough to cast it away. He knows me inside out and I know not much of him. Leaving me for another taught me a lesson in life: to never trust another. From that day on I began to toy with boy's hearts and break them unevenly.

"What's on your mind?" Christopher slowly whispered in my ear. "You." I replied. "But I'm right here." "I'm thinking of the inside of you—your soul and mind." "O...kay." His cologne set me in a sensual mood and so did the recent bathroom scene. "What's that you're wearing?" I asked as I sniffed on his collar. "Hugo Boss." Lovely—a boy with taste.

"Do you enjoy the works of Shakespeare?" He whispered. This was irrelevant to our discussion, but it was exceptional. "Yes. Hamlet in particular." "That's the story of my life." He said. I pulled my head back in confusion, "how so?" I asked. "All of the complications; commotion; romance and betrayal." He said. "Oh, I see." "Do you have a boyfriend?" I looked at him and asked "do you want to be him?" I joked but he took it seriously. "If you'd let me." My lips were then sealed with a sudden kiss. This was too much for one day and night; at first the sister and now the brother. I slightly pushed him away. "Chris—stop it." I muttered.

"You need someone." He said as he pulled me close "You think?" "Maybe. I could be there for you." I then rested my hand on my forehead and sighed. "You can't." "Give me a chance." "No, you don't understand—I'm a puzzle." He then smiled. "No really. I can't validate myself and I sympathize with those who try." And then he said something spectacular:

"I'd regret dying without trying to solve this puzzle for dying itself is a puzzle we sympathize with. Will you sympathize with me?"

"From Hamlet?" I asked. "No, from Christopher." Such perfection in his choice of words, almost as if he recited it somewhere. We kissed.

"Cow." Hariett mumbled as she walked past us. "I really think I should go now. My father's probably worried." "Alright." Hariett said. But she refused to leave, at first, and then Christopher forced her into the car after the hustle. "Why must you drink so much?" Christopher asked Hariett. "Because I can—what were you doing *kissing* her?" Christopher glanced at the rear-view mirror and replied, "because I can." I giggled with my hand covering my mouth as if I was afraid of Hariett. The ride home was awkward—nobody spoke at all until we arrived at my home; it was only then that I heard, "goodnight."

I shut the door and walked inside. Thoughts of tonight wandered my mind....Another nightmare I had to overcome. I assumed that seeing them again was a possibility since I still have her dress, and we'll be going to Egypt together. The weather was fine—nothing special tonight.

*"We then laid there in utter silence…
it was beautiful—it was love. Finally."*

"Where were you all this time?" The vibration in his voice was the second sound I heard after the door shut. "Socializing with friends." I replied. He then moved closer to me and rested his hand on my shoulder. "Next time let us know." I hesitantly nodded my light-head as my palms sweated and knees shook. It felt as though an earthquake struck; only he was the quake and then I—the sensitive ground. "I hope you fully understand my compassion." He said. "Yes, I do." I would've explained to him about Hariett's deception, but the fear of being casted away conquered me. Could it be the fear of my past, or the fear of my present that overpowers me? I slowly excused myself as I walked to my bedroom.

What happened in that bathroom? I promised myself to never go back—but there I was. It was barely my fault. It really wasn't... Hariett should've known better, really. Thoughts of Egypt ambushed my mind now—should they really come along? It could happen again. I refuse to be another victim, but I do it to myself. Why must I be so vulnerable to those I know nothing of? Amanda, where is she when needed most? There was a sudden knock on my door, "come in" I yelled. It was Martin, I forgot about him for a minute. "Did you have fun?" "Yes—I've missed you!" he joked. "Me too… I was wondering where my gossip partner was." he joked. We both laughed as I instinctively began to tear. "What's this?" "I don't know anymore." I said as I sat on the side of my bed. "If what, Beverley?" "If I deserve to live." He then moved closer and whispered, "your beauty can heal the world! Kill yourself and there would be nothing left here."

I understood his intention and I appreciated it. He moved closer and pecked my left cheek with his luscious full lips. I could've sworn that my heart skipped a beat. "Tell me?" He said. "It's complicated really." "I understand complicated." he said. So did I, but I couldn't risk telling him. "Oh it's just my period." I joked. "Aha." He swiftly patted my lap and said, "Take it easy, alright? We can't afford to lose a diamond." He then exited my room leaving me quite happy… happier than I was ten minutes ago.

All I want to do is sleep now, but I was scared. I came here to find my father, and yet here I am kissing girls in the bathroom. I'm insane, but I was told that 'insanity leads to success.' I never really understood that saying, but I'll just pretend that I do. It could've been a mistake to invite Hariett to Egypt but it's too late now. I then received a message from *her* and it read, "great kisser by the way." How sickening. For a second I doubted her cruelty but I was wrong. "Still highly drunk?" I replied. There wasn't another reply from her after that one.

I rested my head on the pillow and reminisced of the days nothing mattered—the days when all I had to do was play with dolls and eat my food. Having disloyal friends never crossed my mind then. The dark days—the bl—blind days. But today nothing is equivalent to the past and I guess that's the reason for the future. "Is Egypt still on, darling?" Hariett suddenly asked in her message. I then felt a sudden dilemma followed by a migraine. If I decline then I'd lose a friend. If I agree then I could still lose a friend. "I think so." I replied. "Great. I'll be over again tomorrow and we can talk about itinerary." Again? My desperation in wanting loneliness was shameful. Ironically, I've felt this way before and I knew what had to be done. Amanda would've known too.

I remember Friday as the day my mind utterly froze. Images of former activities—incidents really, blocked everything irrelevant from staining my mind. The irrelevant things were Hariett and anything related to—Hariett. The whole day was spent like this—nothing else was important. It was Friday and I couldn't ask for more. A nightmare I cherished although I knew that an escape would approach. 'Bed.' That was my word of the day. I heard knocks on the door but I failed to respond. For most; a feeling so heartless only meant one thing... suicide. I needed more days like this. Days that I could understand myself—how strange. At times I would evacuate my bed only to stare at the mirror—rest assured that that face still existed.

I refused to fantasize of Egypt, almost as though I knew it would be cancelled...cancelled? Another door-knock and I had to respond. "Are you alright?" Martin asked as he stared around the dark room. The only light that was noticed was from the crack-opened window. "Yes." He shut the door and walked toward me. "I know I'm not your best-friend, but you can tell me." I removed the cover from my head and stared at him. "Can I?" He nodded. I nervously shook my head—it can't be *that* serious; I should just tell him. I gladly watched him open my curtains since he rescued me. "Your father is out again." I quickly sniffed myself with uncertainty while he stared out of the window. "Are you hungry?" he asked. "Honestly, I am." Before rushing into the bathroom I yelled, "Omelet and pancakes!"

While I was in the shower, I realized something awkwardly pleasing. I think I'm attracted to Martin—awkwardly. After I was clean and prepared to socialize, I quickly checked my Facebook, just in case Amanda sent me something. Naught…So much of a friend to not even notify me on anything. Naught was how I felt for our friendship right then, and I was afraid that feeling would last forever. However, I did receive a request from Lindsey since I couldn't add her the last I tried—how interesting. A message too. "We need to talk." We haven't had a proper conversation and yet she needs to *talk* to me. I accepted her request in hope for a new and, maybe, better friend—thoughts of Amanda escaped my mind, suddenly. "Beverley, your food is almost finished." Martin said as he smiled at me. I stared at him and, unbelievably, seductively licked my lips. What's happening to me? It seemed as though gaining *sight* of things has driven me insane in a way.

Didn't I learn my lesson from last night? I guess not. "Do you still want to know my problem?" I asked him. He then approached me, flirtatiously. "Yes." I remained seated. I stared at him while he tilted his head almost as though he was observing a portrait. Suddenly we kissed... I'm oblivious to how and exactly when, but it happened. A memorable kiss, indeed. I paused and focused on his eyes—his beauty was exquisitely definite. Suddenly his hands rested on my shoulders and I knew that was it. His skin was silky soft and his cologne—heavenly.

Words were not enough although actions were left. Such a beautiful moment that couldn't be elaborated, but I will say that it will never be forgotten...ever. We made love and everything else. Sigh. We then laid there in utter silence... it was beautiful—it was love. Finally.

We then jumped in fear at the sound of a door-knock. Martin jumped out of the bed and ran into the bathroom— rather fast actually. It was Layla, and she had my food with her. "I'm sorry to disturb. Lunch is ready, Beverley."

She must've reckoned the smell in the bedroom—the sex smell always left behind... after sex. I could sense her pretense as she walked away, but I was thankful Martin hid. "Are we safe now?" he asked as I giggled. He then walked to me and kissed my lips. "That was beautiful." I already knew that but another compliment felt good. I watched him as he quickly got dressed. Was that all that he wanted? Just sex... "I want to stay, but I can't." I understood it as much as my heart hurt. "I know." I said. Another kiss was anticipated—and then fulfilled; everything felt gratifying—in the moment—sweet.

That was it. He returned to his job and I was left in bed… almost like a housewife or a mistress. I regret—not knowing why. But something was wrong. Was it him or me? Either way; I didn't feel pleasant at that moment. I lacked excitement and the glee that most would feel after an extravagant experience—wild sex. Either way, I knew something majorly wrong was to happen. Everything I touch and love must be defaced—why? I've failed to find an answer to that, but I hope I do soon. I'm beginning to regret life and that's quite absurd really.

I can't seem to grab the hints thrown at me from all the mistakes I make, but I feel trapped like a Gorilla chased in the mist of some sort. I remember that movie "Gorillas in the Mist" quite well; it's rather pathetic that I'd refer to myself as a Gorilla—they know better. Anyway, trapped is what I was and I needed an escape. Every turn I seemed to take lead to a catastrophe—different and complex issues that a human cannot face alone.

Lonely is what I was, at the moment, at every moment. I ask of too much in life, and whatever I receive never seems to be enough for me—absurd really. If you've ever been in a similar situation; just keep in mind that everything happens for a reason. I like to say that: 'behind every storm prevails a rainbow,' and it's quite ironic how I can't live up to my own expectations…everything is too much of a stormy day for me. If all fails, slit a wrist—some say. I might as well live up to that since my issues are and were intolerable.

There I laid—naked; constantly oblivion to my past when something intriguing took place in the present.

Here I was, just a naïve girl waiting for a better reason…A better meaning to this viral bug that we all call life.

Another shower was needed—thoroughly, after my lunch. I returned to my Facebook only to find another message from Lindsey—and AMANDA. Amanda was worried and still missed me, as usual. Lindsey: I added her number and rapidly sent a message. "What's the matter?" I waited for a while before I was confused by her reply. "Nothing is as it seems. Hariett really isn't." She must've forgotten to complete it, but I felt highly confused. "I'm sorry?" I replied. "Can we meet today?" Alright, I felt Goosebumps at the moment but who wouldn't? She obviously wanted to speak of Hariett but I'll be with her today. Which is more important now though? I sent her my address anyway. "I promise that what I have to say is vital."

It must've been.

I managed to convince Hariett not to come-over. All I had to do was await Lindsey's words. That was the moment I needed Amanda's advice more than ever, really…

And I couldn't refrain myself from consisting of mind-brawling thoughts regarding Martin. Where he was and what he did mattered—suddenly. I felt the need to call him. I needed to know his every-move. Martin understood me, or so I thought. We had undeniably intriguing chemistry that made me feel *alive*. If his feelings were equal then everything would be sane. For a moment nothing else mattered; just him and I. If he would return to London with me I would be content. Just content. I couldn't seem to remember the last time I felt alive—or sanely content for that matter.

My mind was self-destructive too, all because of my own actions. No one made me do anything, but then again Hariett was quite a bitch that night…a whore, and I was her conformist slave. The problem with life is that we love the sweet things. The artificially sweet sugar coated things are the ones we seem to be subservient to. We love it. We appreciate anything that makes life easy for us—and in my case, and at the moment, it was Martin. I'm oblivious to his entire history but that fact, alone, made that all the more interesting.

Love. It's an alias to a defaced mind—a confused mind. I don't really want love, my mind is confused as it is. But love doesn't know that. Whether you're ready or not; it will surely slap you in the face, and you will fall. Love. I remember what it did to me, I refuse to forget. But Martin—my new devotion has left me alone already.

My life is a twisted saga. It would be a book that won't be put down, and it would be unforgettably dramatic. I've been through it all—from love to death and suicidal intents. Nothing and nowhere is safe. I reminisce on the days my dolls were important—nothing else. Everything I did back then wasn't risky. Everything had a consequence but, back then, I was an exception. I always had a way out…always. Sometimes I wonder whether that's the reason for my downfall—the fair share of pain and happiness.

Others close their eyes and envision happiness, while I paint a clear image of failure. I've tried to succeed, but my attempts were not enough…they never are. If there's one thing I learnt from living its that every breath you take could be the last. Hariett was a mistake—she was. I was *good* before she came, right? I was *nearly* there! I thought she 'understood' me but I was wronged. That's another lesson to learn: don't trust anybody—sometimes not even your conscience—in my case.

I feel stupid actually—as usual. I confided in them with my heart, and even that wasn't enough. What wrong have I done? I felt betrayed and what hurt the most was that a stranger betrayed me. Mother warned me about strangers—to never talk to them. I chose to confide in them. It wasn't completely my fault though—they were artificially sweet. That's what we love the most.

My phone rang and it was Lindsey. "I'm by the gate," she said. My palms then began to sweat. All because of curiosity. "I'll be down in a bit." I quickly brushed my hair and ran downstairs. Before I could run out the door I found her there, in front of me. She wore her worn-out jeans and black tank top…she looked good. She reached for a hug, but I didn't want to. She received the 'butt out' hug I guess, nothing too mutual. "How are you?" "I'm *good*. You?" "Perfect, but not so…" confused girl. "Are you thirsty or hungry?" I asked. As much as I needed her to gossip I had to reveal hospitality there and then. "Water." She said. We walked to the kitchen and then *it* began.

"When was the last time you've *seen her*?" I directly assumed she was referring to Hariett since she had something to say about her. "Hariett." I said before I cleared my throat. "Last night." "Really?" she shrieked.

I nodded. "Everyday?" "No. We were together on Wednesday and yesterday."

She quickly grabbed my hand and whispered, "they are evil." "Evil?" I asked. "Hariett knows exactly what she's doing. I tried to warn you. Remember at the Embassy?" "No I don't *remember*." "When I told you that *we* should hang out again." How was I supposed to know that was a warning—I'm not a *psychic*—not that I know. "But—" I hesitated. "It was a warning Beverley. Now look what's happening!" "But, I didn't say anything yet. Nothing happened." I tried to defend Hariett and myself, but she wouldn't buy it. "It's written in your face—in your eyes." "What?" "What happened?" she asked. I figured that there was no point in hiding it.

Before I could open my mouth, I remembered the threat. If I were to tell a soul I'd be dead. I don't want to die yet. I stared around the kitchen in hope that Musa was nowhere near… And thankfully he wasn't. "See, you know what I'm on about." She said. "No. I don't." "Then why so nervous?" I wasn't. She let go of my hand and leaned back on the chair. "I'll tell you a story. Maybe it will loosen you up." What is she up to? Before she began I already thought her story was bullocks. Utter gibberish.

"Promise you won't tell a soul though!" I *understood* what she meant. "I promise." "Last year, we went to the club." I already knew what's next—Hariette did to her what she did to me. "Hariette made me do things." I stood up and said, "things like?" "Just things… you know." "No, I don't know." I said. It took her a while to confide in me.

You could tell she was afraid—threatened…intimidated child. She then took a deep breath, and said…

"She kissed me and—" I nodded my head as a signal for her continuation. "well—she also then fingered me and the rest." "The rest?" "Yes, I'm certain you know what." Wow. So it could be true. Hariette could really be evil—sick or just a psychopath of some sort. To think that I invited them to Egypt—disgusting. "There's more." She continued. I sat down. "After we were done, she told me to never tell a soul. And then after that Christopher asked for a dance. I forgot to mention that Harriett got me completely drunk—loads of tequila; *they* managed to get it into this club—and such." My jaws then dropped.

There was an awkward silence, followed by sounds of footsteps. She left. If only I trusted her.

I tried to pretend as though this was all new to me—but this was sick. It was insanity at its worst. Something had to be done.

"Something has to be done." She said. I quickly nodded. "This is evil." "I tried to explain to you, Beverley." "I wanted to tell you before, but I was afraid. You know, Hariett has her ways." I said. "Yes she does." She said as she gulped down her water.

It was suddenly silent. We both stared at each other and then away—we knew there really was something wrong… but we were afraid. The thought of Hariett sickened me but I wasn't certain. What if Lindsey was lying? I also kissed Hariett back—but she got me drunk. This was an ultimatum…a crazy one. "Do you understand now? This is why I refuse to spend time with them. The other day at the Embassy was coincidental—I never knew they were back." "No. But you had to pretend as though it was alright." I said. "Listen, be careful. Don't tell anybody anything." "But nothing happened to me." I yelled. "So something did happen to you." She must be deaf. "No!" I yelled. "Yes—I can tell." "What do you think happened,

Lindsey?" "The exact same thing that happened... to me."
She whispered.

"Right?" I finally gave in. "Yes. Something happened
last night." I continued. She then closed her eyes and
sighed. "Go on." she said. "Well, from what I remember: I
confided in them. I told them my deepest—some secrets."
She then interrupted me with, "Ditto!" "Anyway, like I
was saying: I told them stuff, and then they insisted that
we should go clubbing. We got dressed, and then we
went." "And then?" "Well—she made me fake my age
to enter and then the tequila shots followed up. I mean,
aren't we in Sudan? I thought alcohol was a bit—difficult,
to get around here. Anyway, afterward, we ended up in
the bathroom; kissing and stuff—and then the threat
followed by a dance with...Christopher."

"I knew it!" she said. "Just pretend to be completely
oblivious, please." "Hey, we are on the exact same boat,
Linds." "Now what?" "Now nothing. It's a secret."
"Listen—there's one other thing." "Oh God." She said. "I
invited them to a trip with me to Egypt—for Christmas."
"Cancel it. They can't go! And *I* was not invited?" "They
said that your head was buried in books." "As usual."
"Cancel it." She continued. "I can't just—no, I won't, it
was a surprise from my father...yeah."

She scratched her head vigorously. "Lice?" I joked.
"No. I'm just nervous." If that's her reaction to nervous-
ness then I don't want to know anything else. "She was
coming today—to speak about Egypt." I said. "Please
tell me you said no." Lindsey said as she pulled her hair.
"Yes. No. I said no." "Thank God." I never understood

how cruel people could be and I'm not certain I ever will. "This is sickening." I said. "Tell me about it. But hey, which secrets did you speak of?" "Just secrets." "We can switch if you want—I'll tell you one and then it's your turn." "I don't think we—" Lindsey then interrupted me: "I was raped once. The hardest secret, but I've learnt to deal with it." I'm not alone. There's someone else who can share my pain—but not quite. "I'm so sorry, Lindsey. When?" "Years back. A stranger in the alley."

"What were you doing in the alley?" I quickly asked. "Drunk—my friends ditched me." Her 'so-called friends' she meant. "Yeah, I never really blamed anyone but myself." she continued. "Blame yourself? Why?!" I laid my hand on her shoulder. "Because I was drunk." "No, you don't blame yourself for that. You blame yourself for stealing candy or money—not rape." I then broke-down. "Why are you crying?" she asked. I wiped my nose and stuttered, "it-happened-to-me-too."

"Are we one in the same? Is this all a sign?" I failed to reply. "Mine wasn't a stranger." "Then who did it?" she asked. "I—" My father then entered the kitchen from nowhere. "Shunu yaha bibti? What's this?" He asked as he leaned in to see my face. "Bas nefsu mush'killah kul shahr." Lindsey said. I never knew she spoke Arabic. "Oh—wallahi? Ok. Sorry ya habibti." He said as he patted my shoulder. "Ana Lindsey." She said as she stuck her hand out for a shake. "Salam! Ana Philip!" "Ahlan musahlan!" I hardly understood the diction thrown around, but I knew it was safe... I thought it was.

> **Shunu:** What
> **Bas nefsu mush'killah kul shahr:** The same monthly problem
> **Ana Lindsey:** I am Lindsey
> **Ahlan musahlan:** Hello (Greetings)

It's hard to trust—anything and anybody now. As I stared at Lindsey I found myself wondering whether she really is Lindsey—just Lindsey. I've learned that most people really aren't who they say they are...who and what they portray can just be another act. I was highly referring to Hariett and her Grim brother, Christopher. I've always suspected her, but nevertheless, I failed to prove my instincts. If there ever was a fool—an idiot who failed to understand deception; then that would be me. I'm not quite a saint myself judging by my actions last night, and today of course. Will there ever be a day when Hariett conquers all vulnerable minds? I highly believe so. The *bitch* conveys nothing but demonic intents. "You don't believe me?" Lindsey mumbled. I quickly turned my head and said, "I do." Lindsey was my evidence here... my alibi. She's been through something quite equivalent. I shrugged my shoulders as I continued to stare at her. As usual, father exited the house—again. I demanded to know his profession. His constant flee was senseless and rather irritating. Did he not appreciate my presence? I failed to understand all of it. "I know how you feel. Betrayal really does sting, but please bear with me." she continued.

If only Lindsey was here before all of this... things would be different. But then there I was, infront of the harsh truth that fed on my heart and mind. I should've stayed in London. It wasn't safe there—but it's all I probably had, really. Mistakes were made but I've learnt from each one—I swore to myself. I swore to Amanda and to my mother. But there I was. It seemed like a game to me—all of this couldn't be real. If it's a lesson, then I have learnt from it, please end now. If I had the choice to discharge myself from this I would, but I can't. The only control I have over this is to reminisce. Not much of a control but it leaves me with something. Maybe if I tried hard enough—never mind. We've all been in regretful situations but I feel alone. Almost like a soldier left to fight alone at war...impossible.

"*Where are you?*" Lindsey whispered as she waved a hand in front of me. "Here. Nowhere." Lindsey then exhaled as though she were exhausted. With her hands placed on her hips she said, "you know. There is an easy way out." I shook my head. She continued, "they say if you can't beat them; join them." "But—" "But in our case, we *can* beat them. Ignore every action they may conceive of." she said. "I can't play games anymore." I whispered. "It's not a game really. It's more of a battle—only we're set to win." You see Lindsey *was that* soldier and I was intimidated by the fact that I'd leave her to fight alone...I did. "Are you always so scared?" I refused to answer. I only glared at her with my piercing eyes.

"You know—if I had just one wish, I'd wish that Hariett suffered from a long-term disease. Worse than

161

cancer..maybe AIDS." I muttered. "And there I thought that *I* was the evil one." she said. "Why?" "Must you ask? I'm sure that you're well aware." I then wiped the sweat off my face. "If you could kill her—would you?" she asked. "Aha, one of those rhetorical questions." "No. It's an actual question." "Yes I would, and then I'd crucially burry her as well as spit on her grave." I said. *How harsh.* "You would too." I continued. "No, I wouldn't." "Nonsense." "Before I'd conceive of such a thing, they would kill me first." She said. Lindsey then cleared her throat and whispered, "that's the secret." I never quite understood where her mind wandered.

"Trust me." she said as I laughed in my heart. "Trust me, Beverley." "Why? I trusted *them* and now look where it got me." I whispered back. "Yes but I'm not them. I'm myself." "Exactly!" I yelled as I turned my back toward her. There was an awkward silence followed by sounds of footsteps. She left. If only I trusted her.

I was left alone again. Here's a secret: I've always suffered from delusions and I'm beginning to wonder if all of *this* was just another illusion. I know the pain is real and so is Hariett. The feeling was the problem—it seemed painful but unreal. I needed answers now, but I fear that I'd never receive them. Everything is happening too fast. I've only just arrived and yet it feels like forever. I really don't approve of trouble but when I'm facing it I can't seem to handle it—it handles me. I'm not weak or anything, I'm just...confused now. Martin. I need Martin. Amanda more than Martin now. I needed her advice—again.

The night swiftly ended without much, of interest, done. I found myself almost asleep...alone again. What have I done byfar? Made new *friends*, I went shopping, and then out. That's it—it felt like I was in London. Suburban London. I used to be good. I followed the rules, I honestly did. I grew up well and in a clean neighborhood. Everyone watched over each other. That was the way. Each mistake was jotted down to prevent you from the next. It really was an adequate life that I lived. It wasn't until I met Amanda. Such a close friend she was—a good friend, I thought. There wasn't a thing that we've never encountered. We were always together. Best friends forever was the promise.

People called me crazy and a delusional. But I wasn't. When man can't see or hear the same as you; they directly call you an immorallychallenged being—maybe not in person. That's what *they* were. But perhaps they were correct. Being temporarily blind must have been the reason. You see, I lost sight of things at birth, that wasn't my fault. We never knew why, but then my life changed. Everything seemed senseless, then. That's when I began to keep secrets and do things—despicable things. I was alone and I was desperate for an exit. A quick way out was all I needed. That's when I met Amanda. Being nineteen was when I was, definitely, introduced to bad. I didn't know much. I didn't care of consequences just as long as we had fun. It got us far—but not positively. Amanda knew the rules, but it was too late.

Mother never really gave consent—she never knew Amanda. I failed to understand that. She was jealous because her friends weren't Amanda. Mother always wanted things for herself, she never accepted a smile on my face—most of the time. A second mother would be needed—a second chance. Being blind wasn't fun, but it wasn't bad either. People did favors for you and respected you—in a way. It was a different world. A non prejudiced world, with my eyes almost shut like that. At times I'd pretend to smile not knowing that I was fooling the world—and myself. When they see you smile they assumed that nothing was wrong meanwhile you suffered alone. But Amanda saw right through me. She knew my every move and so forth. Amanda was everywhere and anywhere I was. She was like the wind; the air; the water. She was like a conscience to me.

Sometimes I wonder where she came from—everyone is from somewhere.

Being blind was something I came to resent. Speaking of it seemed senseless. Blind was nothing in comparison to my present capabilities though; I had it all... I thought. Blind was the reason mother sent me here. She felt as though her responsibilities ran its course, now that I can see. But what hurt her the most was that my father didn't want a blind child. He disowned me and so did his family—it's what I was told. My mother grabbed me and fled the country—it's all coming back to me now. She fled, and all I could hear was Arabic and airplanes. *I was here* and I've smelled this air before. I've touched the ground that I was caged from. She kept me away from the truth but it's too late now. I know things but I lacked what I really *needed* to know. Who *is* my father?

If I asked Martin, maybe I would've known. I chose to remain quiet, just for a while. Maybe it's better if I remain oblivious to the truth, at least in my own way. I could pretend that Philip is my father. I'm good at that. But I could pretend that I'm blind. No, not that. To sit and wait for the result was all that I could do, for now. Amanda. Where was she when I needed her the most? At times I'd wish to be in a secluded island, faraway from pain. If only life was controlled by every thought; want; need; desire—without reckless motives. There are days when I'd shut my eyes and it would be like before—darkness. I'd be blind again for a while. I resent those days but I would never change anything if I could. Life works in a strange way, and it's only the good things that we remember—the rest are only yesterday's trash.

At times I find that I'd question myself: Questions that I can't seem to answer. *Why me?* There are days when confusion alters my mind. There was nothing I couldn't do without a push from trouble. There was nowhere I could go without a path to trouble. Alone. That's where I am. Solitude is who I've become, or who I always was.

Most children dreamt of material things, but I didn't. I was different—I was a challenge. I dreamt of change. Something that was quite unpredictable. I was just always different really. Never was I special, and never was I important. Like a child left to rot; was how I felt. Only

I was a blind child... a special child was how I felt about myself. Nobody else felt this way, except for Amanda. Being blind was a daily battle which I won...eventually. Maybe I was too busy being blind that I've forgotten who I truly am. I couldn't have *just* been a blind girl introduced to Delinquent. I was more than that but I couldn't seem to justify *that* to myself. I'd lay on my bed and stare at the ceiling. For the first time my mind was blank. Just like the ceiling. For the first time I actually felt normal, but it wouldn't last.

I remember being sent off to the best doctors— psychologist and psychiatrists. The best. But sometimes the best isn't good enough—I remained a delinquent. It seemed as though blindness kept me from positive actions as well as observation. Trouble—I am.

"I refuse to be the dog that will run toward a non-existent bone."

No sight of Martin. I was beginning to feel nervous and oblivious as to why. Maybe he quit, or maybe the sex was bad. There could be a thousand maybes but only he knows the answer. I could spend days wondering why, but I'd never know... I'm a loser. I lose everything I have; before I could truly have it. I would say that love is blind but then again so was I. Maybe if I were to confide in him would he then sympathize for me. But this was not love. No, this was not love at all. Today was different. Unlike yesterday I felt—just different. A hot shower before anything else was needed. But alcohol was suddenly desired by me. The steamy water never embraced my body like this. I felt endearment and light-weighted. Just like before. Before I tumbled on the ground. London, I'd never forget you. It's with you I belong and with you I'd die. The ground of London took me. It owns me now. Never let me go is a promise it made to me. *Amanda. Never let me go.*

Before I could reach for my towel I heard cries. Not an ordinary cry. My body shivered; my mind paused. What's happening? Layla rushed into my room yelling "it's your father. He's been shot!" I stood there as I attempted to put her words together. "Shot?" "Yes. Martin is with him at the hospital." "Is *he* alright?" Frankly, my emotions were fucked. I cared, but I worried more about Martin. I couldn't let *her* know that. "Are they alright?" "Yes." I quickly sighed and asked if I could see them. "No. Your father is worried. He needs you at home." I failed to understand why but it made sense. I stayed home. My mind was scattered and I couldn't stop shaking. What if he knew of Martin and I? He would get sacked— because of me. I wished that Martin would return with me. He wouldn't have to be a chauffeur. He could have more opportunities. He would've been somebody and I would've tried to help him—since I can't help myself.

Harriett then rang and insisted that I'd go out with her. I declined and so she invited herself over. I couldn't resist, otherwise she would know. The truth would be so transparent. We couldn't let *them* know. It was a secret. Yet another secret. I wasn't shocked by her quick appearance. It was Hariett. Never have I acknowledged such a creature—A monster actually. A brutally, almost disowned, monster that needed to be left alone. Alone, almost like me. Christopher in the other hand, I have not yet quite observed? He might as well require an equivalent definition... monstrous.

There she stood, with her knee-high boots and skinny jeans (just like Samantha). Her overly brushed hair and those piercing eyes. That transparent top can't fool me. She opened her mouth and exhaled, "it's been a while." Almost as though she knew my intention. So what if she knew? It wouldn't quite differ...I had to eliminate her from my life. Her and that brother of hers. "Yes." I replied while staring at the landscape outside. I had to avoid eye contact. "What-do-you...want?" "Do you hate me already? I'm sorry about the other night, but I was drunk." She said. That's what they all say. "But I know you enjoyed yourself—because I did." she continued.

I quickly stared at her in denial, but I couldn't say anything. "I wanted us to discuss Egypt." she mumbled. "Where's Christopher?" I quickly asked, hoping to change topic. I tried to stay off of that subject—Egypt was not for *us*. "Busy." she replied. I felt dumbfounded by her reply, but I knew it was a lie. Christopher is hardly busy—since I've known them. "About Egypt. It's cancelled." I lied as her jaw dropped as if I offended her mother. "My father has important business plans. Very vital." "I'm sure. Why didn't you inform me?" "I just did." "BEFORE." she yelled.

So, Lindsey was absolutely and utterly correct about Hariett. She has to have what she wants right there and then. But I refuse to be her conformist. I refuse to be the dog that will run toward a non-existent bone.

"Oh. So I might as well leave now?" She said as she vigorously swung her bag on her shoulder. If that was a rhetorical question, I think I'd die laughing in my heart. "Well?" I guess not. "If that's why you're here then I suggest you leave...no offense." "Non taken. Good-bye." she roughly turned toward the gate and marched away like a soldier in a 'no man zone.' I sucked my teeth before I shut the door. I frankly *do not care...anymore.*

Hariett. A rare character labeled as a succubus. She feeds on your anxiety...sadist. She reminds me of someone

I once knew. Family actually. They pretend to love you, care and protect you; when they deceitfully lead you toward a fire. The raging fire that conquers her—only to be put out by the depression of others. Pain...that's what *they* love. When I was younger I never quite understood this raging fire within. Maybe because I couldn't see. But now I'm not quite certain whether life has ever been as pristine. My heart aches. My mind is sorrow. My soul... nothing in comparison to yours.

I've learned to be adequately strong. I've learned from the best. Even though there were days when suicide wandered my mind; I've learnt to seclude it...faraway. Amanda. I remember the pain. I could never escape, or at least I thought so. I've escaped. But only after my energy, pride and integrity were raped from me. Darkness was my life...just darkness. But it wasn't until I acknowledged Amanda. I miss her. Really.

I've always been taught to speak up, but there are *things* that are meant for silence. I'm sick. The thought of all of this sickens me. My heart aches—agony. My past was darkness. Present—complicated. And my future? bound for negativity. I'm not stupid. I've been told so. I'm not stupid. If ever there was another *war,* I'd be front and center. My strength can be shared. I've gained it back. If you stare at me I may appear weak; strange...disowned. If you only knew the things we've been through; Amanda and I. I conceal it. Silence is for the weak hearted, which I'm not. No I'm not. You might call me paranoid, but there's a certain extent to which someone can endure pain, depression and loss, all at once. I'm strong. I won't let them feed on what is left of me...artificially sweet. There are certain people who search for problems and others who don't. Hariett is one of them—who did. She deserves an award for being a deceptive conceited shit. I can't seem to understand the bad luck that I possess...why me? The anger that grows within me cannot be contained...I try but I always fail. Failure.

I was afraid that insomnia would alter my life, again. It used to before... I was never strong enough to defeat it, I always needed somebody there. Too many thoughts can lead to a defaced mind...a defaced you. But I never quite learned *that*—I was focused on Amanda. I mistreated myself, just because others fail to understand me— except for Amanda. She understood everything. She was everything I had... I thought.

I want to go home. If I could flee then I would—but I'm on a mission. I could just deliberately sicken myself and ask for mother...they would send me back. But then it would be a waste of time—of everything. I'll just wait. "Beverley!" yelled my *father*—Philip. I ran toward his voice as though to save him from death. "What's wrong?" I gasped. After a long and depressing pause, he stuttered; "About Egypt—" he cancelled it. It's not happening anymore. "Are your friends still with us?" he continued. I sighed and then shook my head. "Just us— that's even better." "Alright then. How is your friend?" he asked pretending as though I didn't know about his accident. "Lindsey?" "Yes." she wasn't a friend—she was more of an acquaintance who possessed information. A lot of adequate information. "Good." he said. "I promise, we'll spend more time in Egypt. What's for today—shopping?" my eyes lighted up like a bulb. "Hmmm. Yes." He reached into his pocket and handed over the credit card. For the first time, ever, I've managed to touch one. Mother never trusted me with one. It felt good—it's very *healing*. It was a remedy. "Thank you." I hugged him. "Your grandmother is coming. Either today or tomorrow—that one is unpredictable." he said as he laughed. "Eat something. You look skinny." Do I, really? I loved the thought of being skinny, finally.

"We need to talk later. Don't leave the house." he said and then stared at me and shook his head: "go eat, please." He then waved goodbye and then I thought of something...it was depressing. What if one day, I never see him again? He never bothered to mention the shot. He leaves his credit card, but not his love. I'm not his own—I'm not his blood? At least I thought so...

Still, no word of or from Martin. I really miss him now. *Is he sick? Dead*—no it can't be. Was I too much of a tramp? Maybe he travelled—*maybe everything*. I quickly glanced at the gate only to find someone else; another chauffeur. It wasn't Martin—definitely not. Who was this stranger? He was the complete utter opposite of Martin. Not a toblerone—my toblerone. A minute later I found that I had shed a tear, without knowing. It hurt too much. It was different. I felt real—and important, somehow. I needed the answer right then. Where is Martin? For a second I thought he was on vacation—*wrong*. I rushed to Musa, our chef, and asked him. He was preparing lunch but I still interrupted. "You mean you don't know?" he said. I then felt my heart skip a beat. My tummy; knees; hands—weak. "What?" He then moved closer and whispered, "Martin quit." My eyes quickly shut in disbelief. We were together yesterday. It wasn't a relationship but it was something real—it was special to me. "But—" "He never said why." Musa said. "But my father never told me." "Your father..." he said after a pause. "Yes?" "Martin *just* quit." He continued. I felt as though I were the clown. The joke within this house. I failed to understand the betrayal—but he'll come back.

Could *that* have been what Philip needed to discuss? Maybe Martin confided in him, but I doubt it. He wouldn't do that to me—*us*. I spent the day thinking of why he left me, where he was and what he did. It was insanity—I was in love with a stranger...almost. Was it done to hurt me or save me—*save himself?* I'm certain of nothing. Not even myself anymore.

All I knew was that I was badly hurt. Like a child falling on some hard ground; I'm hurt. I over-exaggerated the situation but it still *did* exist. Like a permanent scar left to heal—never. I still needed an explanation. A clear elaboration of his actions...why? I could be stubborn but then again I slept with the man. A man. He wasn't my first but he was different. It reminded me of a man who loved me—back in London. He really loved me. Brian—a boy actually. Anything I wanted was offered to me— pizza I mean. He never understood me but he strived to acknowledge my character. *Fail.* Martin understood me—or not.

Amanda called him my Pizza-sugar-daddy." Which he was not, but I still questioned myself sometimes. His name was Brian. The story of how we met was rather interesting—juvenile. Amanda ordered Pizza and he delivered it. You know this already. Why repeat.

Brian, I had to let him go. I needed more than *he* could offer.

Sunday ran its course and my curiosity nearly strangled me. Before I tied a rope around my neck there was a phone-call. It was Martin. The sound of his voice gave me a fiery intensity of feeling. I just loved it. "Beverley, something is wrong." Oh no, here it comes. "It's our father..." he paused almost as if to deliberately create a dramatic effect. "What?" All I heard was *'our'* father but I was certain it was a mistake. "He was shot again." he continued. My jaw dropped and I felt the quick drum-ish beating of my heart. I could hardly breathe. The word: 'again,' repeatedly crossed my mind. I wanted to puke— nausea. "Is he..." he then quickly interrupted, "alive." I grasped on my heart almost as if to shield it. "I'm at the hospital right now—but the driver is dead." I then began to cry as I envisioned his death as opposed to the death of the new chauffer. 'Thank God—I mean it wasn't you, thank God." my words were quite senseless.

"Grandmother is on her way to you." I needed someone with me—I felt so unsafe. Who shot Philip *again*? *Why*? "She'll tell you *everything*." he continued. Are they after me now? Never have I encountered such fear—I was ready to flee. "Everything will be alright." he said. "What happened?" "I don't exactly know." "But then how..." I said. "I was told." Martin replied. There was something he wasn't telling me. Obviously something highly confidential. "Beverley—there's something else. I'm sorry." "Sorry?" "I never knew. Please believe me, Beverley. I'm so sorry, *ya oghti*!" He began to cry, but I was confused. I refused to cry with him. *What was the matter here?* "I have no idea what you're on about." I said as I slammed my foot on the ground. "Please forgive me!" he said. I removed the phone from my ear and then disgustingly stared at it—as though he were observing me. "Why? Were you the shooter?" "No. Just know that I'm sorry. So terribly sorry." I wish I could turn back the hands of time. Remain in London—away from this mess that I've caused. That's all I seem to do really...deface things.

After the call ended I felt something strange. I never felt it before, but it had to go away. I no longer felt love for Martin. It was gone—so quick? Maybe it wasn't love after all. The doorbell rang and I knew it was *her*—she's here to tell me everything. Whatever *everything* was. She ran toward me the instant the door opened. "*Ya habibti*, please come to me." I ran—I walked if you will. I was afraid. She hugged me and stroked my hair as though I were a doll. "I'm so sorry." I would've lost my mind right then and there. All the apologies really left me furious.

"Sit down." she pointed at the sofa. I swallowed my spit and then tried to control my breathing state. "As you know, your father was shot—twice, but he's alive sweetheart. *Al hamdil alah*." I continued to listen while staring endlessly. "There's something else." She continued.

My heart rushed and I felt as though I were to die. This was abnormal. I didn't deserve this. "I told you *not to* fall for Martin. Now *look!*" "Look at what?" I asked. "You *stupid* girl. He—" I shut my eyes as I already predicted the answer. Please don't say it. I spared a quick second to pray to God although I lacked sense of religion—did *He* hear me? "Martin." She said. I clutched my fist and chanted in my mind, *"please God, no."* "He's your brother." she then jumped from the sofa and walked toward the window. "This isn't true. I don't. I don't have a brother—anymore." I stuttered. "You don't know *anything.*" She was right. I hadn't a clue about anything... not even the truth.

Ya oghti: My sister

Alhamdilalah: Thank God

"Your mother sent you here to find your brother, *not your father.* She already knew the truth." She said. But I was confused. "What?" "Before your mother gave birth to you, Philip learnt that Martin wasn't his son. They had an argument and then she ran-away. Never to be seen again." I cuffed my mouth in disbelief. "She knew that he *would* work for Philip—but she had no choice." "Why?" "He had nowhere else to go. His father died and Philip showed nothing but compassion." she said. "She never told me this." "Of course not. She was shunned. She sent you on a mission." she then paused and sadly stared at me. "But Martin knows now—I revealed it today." "No!" I screamed! "No!" I screamed again. She held me and said,

"I'm sorry! I wish—" but then I pushed her back and yelled, "you don't understand—I can't stay here!" I began to cry as thoughts of sex with Martin altered my mind. "No!" I would've stabbed myself if I had the chance...I slept with my brother, I didn't know he was, and even though he looked nothing like me; we were blood. I knew the circumstances but I could never be set to face them.

I felt dizzy—insane. I was at loss for words—could this *really* be? All I knew was that staying here was insidious. I had to leave...right away. "Beverley, *he* confided in me. He told me *everything*." she whispered. My breathing came to a sudden halt. My mind shivered. Everything seemed surreal at this point. Just like in the movies, you know? "Everything like?" I asked. "I know what happened yesterday." I then began to cry. I couldn't help myself. "We all make mistakes. Love is blind, it knows not of religion, race—or in your case; family." she said. It felt as though she meant to threaten me. "Nothing happened." I yelled. "*It* happened. You should've remained bl—" she then stopped. "Blind?" I asked. "Blind? *Is that what they wanted?* "I've spoken too much. The rest is for you." she said. "The rest of what? I never knew okay?" "It shall stay that way." she swiftly walked toward the door as if there was no more to say, and she left...she just left me standing there confused and hurt.

She was right. If only I remained blind. At least I wouldn't *really* understand everything. But I wasn't— I could see everything. Even though I wish that things were never the same. I stood there with a clustered mind— almost frozen. I had a choice to make: to stay or leave immediately. I've been on a mission that was non-existent. I felt stupid, naive and manipulated. Something had to be done, but what? Is that why I hadn't spoken to mother since my arrival? *It could be—I don't know.* Egypt, *what about it? I want to go. But father was shot and Martin is my brother.* I had to flee back to London then, I've missed it...Amanda.

Disgusted. That's how I felt...disgusted. I wondered why mother never confided in me—too many secrets. My life *is* a secret and I wish I remained blind. I assumed that life would change if I gained sight of everything but I was wrong. At times I'd wonder how many breaths it took for it to be the last. I tried to fulfill that theory but I never managed to succeed. I remember when suicide was all I had...it really was. Intentions of jumping off a roof really did calm me, ironically. I'm a strange child and at times I wonder if blindness was the cause of this.

Strange.

"Never again."

I missed the London air; food; water; the life. I longed for the designer clothing and freshly baked croissants too. Tea? They say, 'you never know what you have until it's gone.' I believe it's because London is what I had. It's really all I had...and suicidal intents. I want it back. I couldn't seem to care for Philip—how selfish. He's been shot and yet I only wander of what I could have. Me, it's always about me—I was told. No wonder I lacked true friends and loved ones. Martin—will I ever see him again? Was this the end? Does Philip know of Martin and I? It's rather sickening. 'Martin and I.' With my eyes closed I began to contemplate on the past; future and right now. I hated my life right there and then.

All I seemed to see was betrayal. The only time I ever oozed 'happiness' was during my blind days, when nothing really mattered. I didn't want to reopen my eyes—I loved them this way. Shut. As they remained closed I saw Amanda; far away from me but close to the *actual* truth. She's the only one who knows the truth. It's a secret.

Everything seemed peaceful when shut eyed. I wished to remain. I've never understood why my life was complicated, and still is. I never knew that everything promised was just a lie. Yet another lie. I remember the first lie—I'd never forget. It was a while back after I gained sight of everything that I found a letter on the kitchen counter. It was a letter from my brother, Frederick— written by me, remember? Explaining what *he* had done. I knew what it was but mother hadn't a clue. She stared at me as I stared at the wall. I knew that she wondered whether *I knew*, but I couldn't give myself away. Towards the midst of the letter was when she realized that it was a suicide note. *Frederick had killed himself.* I knew, but I refused to tell mother. It was my secret—Amanda and I.

It was easy to see the pain in mother's eye, but I couldn't show compassion. Not just then otherwise the secret would prevail. I was not ready for that...*she* wouldn't let me. As mother stood there, hoping that it was a prank, I had a phantom grin on my face...almost possessed. Frederick was gone and I knew the answer. The only answer that mother sought.

Amanda stared at me as I grinned but she never questioned me. She always knew my every-move— somehow. She was like a conscience to me. Without her I'd be helpless really. A weakling.

"...Please forgive me. The only thing I regret not telling you is: I love you. I never meant to do this. Life is short, but mine was the shortest. It's better this way, really. You'll soon understand why I chose this road, and I hope you'll find strength to forgive me. I'm sorry...Love, Frederick."

Admiring your own work of art really is a beautiful thing...insane but beautiful. Frederick really had it coming. He never should've done what was done. I didn't know better, but I knew that it was not justified. His actions *really* were shameful. I'll never forget that note—beautiful note. I do miss him really, but I'd rather not think about him—wasteful thinking.

From that day mother never looked at me the same. It was almost as though she knew; but she hadn't known. They say mothers know everything, but *she* was quite oblivious. Even if the truth were to stare her upright; she still wouldn't know anything. "Beverley, Beverley; such a sweet girl. Such a poor blind girl." they would say. Little did they know who Beverley really was. Yes, I was blind and sweet for a while. It wasn't until I caught sight of things that I began to clearly understand life. It wasn't until I kept a secret that I learnt to do bad things. Being blind kept me from certain things, but it also pushed me toward many things. I think I'd be a coward if I weren't blind—thanks to Amanda. At times I'd wonder if I were insane or if it was just everyone else who was.

This is who I'm afraid of being—the person I don't understand. I can't contain myself when I'm her...this. Sometimes it's too late to take back your actions and other times it's too late to react upon an action. I slowly opened my eyes and dealt with whatever came my way. I couldn't hide—shutting my eyes won't change anything. Everything I saw already happened and the more I ran away; the worse it got.

I opened my eyes...back to reality.

"Beverley!" someone yelled at the door. "Come." I said. Layla slowly opened the door as if she feared me. "Is everything alright? Is he okay?" "Yes he is alright—*al hamdil allah*." "Oh, *shukran ya Allah!*" she screamed. She ran downstairs and all I heard was, "*Al hamdil allah!*" I slowly then began to understand that my father was a good man. For his servants to find joy in this news; he must mean something extraordinary to them. I then smiled as I thought of him—my father. I never really accepted him just yet, and somehow, I still failed to believe that he was my father.

Martin rang again that night. We both pretended as though nothing was wrong—as though the truth was well-kept. It was shameful. "He will come home on Monday." he said. I was relieved to learn that Philip would return; although hearing Martin speak killed me inside. His voice slowly grasped my every organ and squeezed them ever so tightly. I couldn't really breathe—but he mustn't know. "Why didn't you tell me?" I asked. "I never knew." "Lies!" I yelled. "Listen to me. You were a blind child and I never knew—that you would gain sight of things. When you came I was never told exactly who you were. We were young when we last saw each other." I began to breathe calmly. "I wish I knew." he continued. "I can't stay here." I said. "You'll just leave? Just like your mother." "Shut up! What do you know about my mother?" "I know that *she is* mine too." I gasped and banged the phone on the wall... just one bang.

"No!" I yelled again with my mouth touching the phone. "Did grandmother not—" "Yes, she explained everything—just like you said." I said as I cried. "Please don't leave—" He can't seem to understand me or the situation I'm in. I wish we never had sex but then again it did happen.

He is my half-brother after all—I suppose we could work things out. "No!" I screamed as I shook my head. Not that he could see it. He remained quiet for a while as I continued to scream. It really wasn't his fault that I couldn't handle the truth.

"Fucking hell!" I yelled, and then I began to cry. "Please don't cry. You're too beautiful to cry." his words only worsened things for me. I wish he wasn't who he was. If only we always received every wish.

"I want to ask you something." I then cleared my throat as a sign for his continuation. "After we had sex—" he then paused in shame. "Go on. Say it. How did you feel?" I tilted my head and said, "trapped." "Alright" he slowly said. "And all sorts of things." "Like?" "Confused and angry. Happy and sad." "Regret?" he asked. "Quiet." and then there was silence followed by, "me too—which is why I quit. I couldn't stand the guilt. I knew that something was wrong the instant I left the house." What was the point of this conversation? Thing's won't change and I'm *still* leaving. I refuse to stay and turn more insane—I won't. "Never again." I said as I hung up the phone. I began to cry again. This is what leads to more confusion and insanity. Why me? That question will remain unanswered, forever...

"Aren't we all, at some point?"

I sat in my room that night, I couldn't dare and bear to step outside. There were only two things left to do: pack my stuff and leave. I would ask myself why bad things happen to good people; but I think I'd rather pass. My eyes were swollen like a recently widowed wife. Such pain in life that some endure...that I can no longer endure. I'd bang my head against the wall but I see no point in it. I'll be with *her* soon. That's all I need...Amanda. I quickly opened my closet and grabbed my suitcase. No, I wasn't leaving today—but the thought of it gave me a rush—a catalyst thing. I grabbed my jeans; shirts and underwear. My every possession had to leave with me...I can't leave a print of memory here. *What a stupid thought.*

I'll explain it to Philip tomorrow—not everything. I'll say something else—a lie perhaps. I stopped moving; almost as though I were held at gun-point and then tears dropped down my cheeks. This was another secret I'd have to keep. Another dark world I must enter—just me. I wasn't certain that I could handle that again. But I had to be strong—I didn't want to be shunned by my family. Again. I then quickly filled up the suitcase—I was set to leave. "What are you doing, Beverley?" Musa asked as he stood there in his apron. "You wouldn't understand." He then moved closer to me and muttered, "try me." I ruffled my hair and sighed. "I can't. I just can't." He closed the door and stood by it. What was he doing? He's supposed to be *in* the kitchen. Cooking or something. "Have you ever kept a secret?" I asked. His head then quickly spun toward me. "Beverley. We all have secrets." Yes, he was right. But some of us just have one too many. "What's yours?" I quickly questioned. "Let's just say that long time ago; I made a mistake." He said. "Well, me too. But it wasn't *that* long ago." "Beverley. You wouldn't understand."

How ironic. I raised an eyebrow and said, "try me." He sighed and pointed at my chair. "Sit there." I stared at his mouth as I anticipated his words. But they wouldn't discharge. I just sat there and waited. All of us enjoy hearing secrets anyway. He placed his fingers on his lower lip and squeezed it. Martin does the same thing; how ironic and coincidental—really. "Hurry, you're making me nervous, Musa." "Okay then—you go first." This became a game of truth or dare. I wasn't in the state for giddiness. "I assure you that mine is worse than yours." he said while I continued to stare at him. "Well...Martin—" he then quickly said, "what about him?" "Well, we did something. Some—umm—errr—just something." He suddenly began to shake. What did I say? I hardly told him what it was. "What do you know?" I asked, and then he exploded. "Martin is my son and he's your step-brother." Stop. Silence. Extreme awkwardness. It almost felt as though I was stomped by a Dinosaur. As though someone yanked out my soul. I felt stupid and used. Insignificant child—I felt unwanted.

A house filled with secrets—a world altered by lies. I needed no more of it. This was just another excuse to leave. A reason desperately needed. I could see it in his eyes—it was dreadful. The pain in his eyes. The hurt. "Your mother—" he slowly said. It was almost as though I was the teacher—him the child or student… and he was in trouble.

"Say no more. Please." I then continued talking as I pushed the top of my suitcase to make space. "Does Philip know?" "No." It did make sense. Philip is always running in and out that he probably couldn't even notice a fire in his home. "You know—secrets come out. Right?" I said.

Why did I torment him with these questions? Who was I to judge? I'm a murderer; thief; liar and many more. Yet I stood there; judging a man who is bound to make mistakes. Who am I?

"I'll just go." Before his hand could reach the door-knob I said, "I'm a murderer; thief and a liar." I then received the most unforgettable response. "Aren't we all, at some point?" I suddenly felt a weight lifted off my shoulders. I felt a sudden peaceful moment. I'm not alone.

I didn't leave my room. I sat there on my bed; thinking. Just thinking. I thought of all sorts of things. Meaningless things and significant things. They were all just 'things.' Nothing was going to change. Nothing really needed to change. *But* how did I get here? I stared at the door hoping for Musa's return. What else was there? As I glanced at my suitcase, with definite confusion, I began to wonder why *this* happened to me—must everything I have be defaced? Why? Was that what I was—a wreck? Or was it that things just *happen*? It's almost as though—as though—I don't know *anymore.*

CHAPTER THREE

Abominable intuitions

Unpredictable trips tend to be more gratifying hence my sudden departure to London. Honestly, I've never learned so much in quicksand situations and short-term social *relationships* as I did in Sudan. And at my current stance I'd only by lying if I labeled my experience: amiss. Little time, big lessons—life has verified its beginning and existence. I've thought of Martin, of Philip, Layla, Hariett, Lindsey, Musa—everything and everyone, yet I couldn't *find* a reason to turn back—to return to Sudan. My potential home at the time of my visit—I thought. I miss the hard-grounds; the heat; food; Arabic—everything. The very essence of Amaraat. I miss it but I resent it, somehow. Am I only being complex? Horrendous? A bitch? The truth (of the matter) is: once you feel discomfort, in any given situation, just flee. Flee without looking back. Flee without regret. Flee by chance and be sure to only obtain your memories. Those are important for later when you're being yanked out of insanity, confusion, and that repulsive and abominable intuition that you use to navigate yourself through life.

Memories. Those are what I have now, now that I've managed to flee from the intolerable—the unmanageable.

My weakness is translucent—and not in a positive enlightening way, I find. As I sit there anticipating my mother's arrival, something hit me—not something solid or anything like that: a clear thought of survival. Maybe focusing on me without having to risk, or sacrifice anything would bring me closer to eternal happiness. That's what I sought: happiness. I've encountered it once or twice and then watched it slip away, yes, I watched happiness slip away. I let it. And there I was practically begging for its resurrection in my life. So I crossed my fingers; squeezed my eyes shut and wished for exclusion from damnation.

Damnation: what a word. I remember it being mentioned once or twice, but never quite thought that I'd think it, let alone utter it, in *my* own life. I'm not any different. I, too, must encounter sour and bitter substances and occurrences in order to appreciate the sweet. I guess I was accustomed to the *bitter sweet*—my own reality. Does that make sense?

My mother soon arrived wearing her red blouse and black pants, as I knew she would. She screamed my name across the terminal and I, somehow, knew that she missed me. But, where was Amanda? I thought she would know everything—where I was and when I'd return. Before I could continue thinking, I heard, "Beverley, ya habibti. There you are!" I walked to her and looked around as she embraced me—I didn't know where to begin. I still felt lost, alone, confused. I felt as though my life ended—it was over, even if my mother was with me now. Amanda wasn't. After resting my luggage in the car, mother asked me many questions—different questions. She was different and it felt as though Frederick never existed—it was gone—her sorrow was..gone. She was completely new—that' s what I thought. It's what I saw. "Tell me everything, Bev." I turned my head and stared directly into her eyes as if I *knew* she knew everything. "Well—". I stopped and thought of what to say. "It was extraordinary, I even made new friends. Phillip—father was really nice to me. Everything felt good. Fine. But—" she then turned her head and smiled. "But I couldn't stand being away from you—from London. From everything here. I had to return." She then nodded and said, "I know. But now I hope that you know what you need to know." It was then silent. No more questions. She just drove us home and I knew this meant a new beginning.

Her eyes had a different look—
almost a different color but not quite.
She was different. Amanda was—not Amanda

"I changed some things here." mother said as she opened the door to our home. Everything was changed, not some of it. It felt different now—new and different. Good. I sighed and continued to walk around as though our home was new to me, I secretly searched for Amanda, maybe she would jump out to surprise me—wrong. "What do you think, Bev?" "I love it. Great! But—" I replied as I threw my bag on the ground and rushed to my bedroom. "I hope nothing has changed." I yelled as I ran. I then flung my door and my eyes opened wider, "nothing has changed." I slowly whispered to myself. The window was there and so was my bed; my chair, mirror; everything. It was left untouched as though I was still here. I ran to the window and swung it open. "Amanda." I cried. "Amanda." But there wasn't a reply.

I turn around slowly hoping that she would be standing behind me, but only my mother was. "Who is Amanda?" she asked as I stared at her in a peculiar way. "Amanda." I said as I slowly pushed her outside and closed my door. I began to cry—not tears of sadness, but tears of relief that perhaps Amanda has found a better friend. A friend who wouldn't destroy—a friend unlike me. "Shh." I quickly turned around and it was her—her—her. "Amanda!" I ran to embrace who I've missed, what I've missed. I ran because I cared, because I loved her. "Bev, where were you? Where *were* you?" she asked as she held my face. "I had to leave—I'm sorry. I had to leave, but I know you were always *with* me." I uttered.

"We have things to discuss, Bev. Things." I then stared at her and suddenly the smile that was on my face slowly vanished. I knew there was something wrong—I lost her although she was right there with me. "Things?" I already planned to tell her everything about my trip, but 'things' definitely meant something else. "Like what?" I asked. "Our friendship. Your trip. Did you really miss me?" she asked. I stood there without a reply, I didn't need to reply. Did I? "Amanda. Of course I missed you. I'll tell you everything, but not just yet." I said. She just stood in silence. "Not just yet?" she asked. "I—feel a bit tired. I really wanted to see you today—I'm so glad you're here!" I said. I then knew that something was wrong—very wrong—very different. Was I gone *that* long. Her eyes had a different look—almost a different color but not quite. She was different. Amanda was—not Amanda.

"Your mind is rushing. Sit down." She said. I then nodded and sat on my bed. "Are you thirsty—hungry?" I asked. She shook her head. "You know, you didn't even have a birthday party. You're eighteen, but you haven't really celebrated *it*, you know?" she said. "Because of everything that happened—it wasn't the time for that—not the right time." I explained. "Bev, what about a small welcome back party and belated birthday party then?" I knew that it was her compassion, but I just returned from Sudan. And even if I were to have a party, who would I invite? "Bev, I'll come—Brian will come. Your mom can be there—maybe your *friends* from school.." she said. "No. They're not friends, I don't know. Where are they now? They aren't friends. And I just came back—I don't know." I said as my neck sunk to one side. "It's already planned. It's supposed to be a surprise party for you." She said as I stood up completely confused. "Who—" "Bev, don't worry about that. Relax." Her words silenced me and all I wanted to do now was sleep.

"I'll leave now. But I will be back." I nodded at her as she slowly drifted away.

When I awoke, I noticed something different—music, at night. I assumed mother had a guest over. I shrugged it off and sneaked off to the bathroom. Suddenly the music stopped and it was completely silent. "Mom?" There wasn't a reply. "Mother?" I yelled. I then slowly walked downstairs, watching each step—my heart was pounding as hard and fast as it did in Sudan. I was afraid. I slowly poked my head to the left and there was nobody in sign. "Mom." I whispered, but didn't receive a reply. As I crept to the living room, my hand on my chest—afraid, I hoped that I wasn't *next*. That death didn't come for me.

"Surprise!" Someone screamed, they were all there. Standing there—with my mother. They planned this and I just stood there in shock. I continued to stand there for a while, before Brian grabbed my hand and lead me to the table where chocolate cake—with mint and nuts—awaited me. I licked my lips and smiled. My head turned left to right—who else was here? "Welcome back. Bev!" mother yelled. I then cried and felt grateful—for the moment. I thanked them for coming—but the best part was Amanda. She was there with her dress—beautiful dress. Waiting for me. I was happy. Content. I was—happy even though the room wasn't filled with people. At least I knew who loved me—who cared. "Bev, this is for you. I'm so sorry for what happened—and I'm sorry about Frederick." Brian said as he handed me a card and an exquisite black rose. "It's amazing—unique really." I said.

We spoke of Sudan, Frederick—everything. But then Brian decided that we needed to enjoy the night—I'm back and that's what mattered. But I didn't know what would follow. Before we could truly dance, and before Amanda could even really speak, the door-bell rang. "That must be *her*." Brian said. Her? Who? Samantha? Does he even know them? As he opened the door, a tall and slim person stood there—she was—his. What was she doing here? "Brian!" I yelled and Amanda whispered that I shouldn't argue. I couldn't bear that he brought someone—his someone to my party. Who was she? Before she was even introduced, I dashed to my bedroom. I dashed as I usually do—dash away from everything. Mother tried to stop me but couldn't—it was all happening again. Again.

The door slammed shut and I felt a shudder of energy flowing out of me—I felt weak and dizzy. The dress that I wore felt useless—ugly. I quickly ran to open my window—I wanted to jump. I had to jump—but I couldn't. "Amanda!" but there wasn't a reply. My body continued to feel weaker, it was as though I was hit by lightning—or something. "Amanda!" and still there wasn't a reply. I inhaled and exhaled and then inhaled again. Staring into my mirror I resented that—this—my reflection. What was I? I slowly began to pull out the rose petals—I didn't mean to harm it. It was beautiful but it was Brian's. But then with every fallen petal, I noticed that my vision began to change—I slowly began to see darkness. Again. "Amanda" I yelled again but without a reply.

Anger then fired my heart, I felt it, I could see it. I began to pull out the remaining petals from the rose, harder and harder, but when I reached the final one Amanda's voice echoed in the room: "As you were when we first met, you shall remain forever."

"Amanda! Amanda help me! I don't understand!" I then turned to my reflection and I was—blind. Blind? My body began to shake, my lips began to quiver. What was happening? I screamed and struggled one last time for Amanda but my voice only weakened—my body felt weaker. "Beverley, this world is not for you, not for us. You don't belong." Amanda said as my body twirled and slammed the ground. Life then began to flash before me—I saw everything. I saw Brian—the rose. I saw him poison it. But why! "I wanted you to know." Amanda whispered. I tried to stand up but I felt "spirit less." My strength in my body was gone.

"This world is just a test for those like us and Brian was your graduation. And this world is forever filled with the artificial sweet, even during the last hours of a delinquent." She said. As my hand touched the ground, I took my final breath only to realize that my rose was gone and so was my life, the life that I wanted, the life that I lived and the life that exited my bedroom window holding my soul hostage.

ABOUT THE AUTHOR

Sabrina Eiya Makein aims to deliver (fiction and non fiction) books for both the Young Adult and Adult readers in various and creative ways. Her work(s) cater to the curious, artistic and imaginative minds. Readers will enjoy her second published book, "Artificially Sweet Delinquent" because it's a psychological suspense thriller novel filled with roller-coaster events, and also because there may be certain areas in this novel that they can relate to as well as various areas, in this work, that the readers can learn from.